“Of c
you must leave him.

Cecily looked down at Jack. He had been carried in on a plank and was now half lying, half resting upon an arm. His pallor was worse than she had expected and her heart went out to him for his bravery.

“My grandfather would not hear of turning him out,” she continued. “And I am certain he will remember his manners once the effects of Mr. Rose’s excellent brandy has worn off.”

But at the sound of Cecily’s voice, Jack had lifted his head and was now focussing his eyes upon her in a curious manner. Suddenly, there was a glimmer in them, as if he had just then recognized her.

He spoke, directing Cecily a look which froze her with embarrassment. “‘But soft! what light from yonder window breaks? It is the east, and Juliet is the sun!’”

Cecily was too stunned to speak. A coachman who quoted Shakespeare! What manner of man was he? The first time she had seen him, she had been struck by the gentleness of his speech. And now this? Could he be a gentleman? Would a gentleman have any reason to drive a mail coach?

Cecily shook herself roughly and ordered the ostlers to carry Jack above stairs to a bedchamber. She watched from a safe distance as the men took him away, but her cheeks blazed a fiery red as his parting words drifted back to her.

“‘It is my lady; O, it is my love! O, that she knew she were!’”

Books by Patricia Wynn

HARLEQUIN REGENCY ROMANCE

THE PARSON'S PLEASURE
12–SOPHIE'S HALLOO
24–LORD TOM

JACK ON THE BOX

PATRICIA WYNN

Harlequin Books

TORONTO • NEW YORK • LONDON
AMSTERDAM • PARIS • SYDNEY • HAMBURG
STOCKHOLM • ATHENS • TOKYO • MILAN

Published November 1990

ISBN 0-373-31138-9

Printed in U.S.A.

CHAPTER ONE

JACK HENLEY, the beloved only son of Sir Geoffrey Henley, Baronet, was standing stiffly erect under the stern scrutiny of his venerable parent's eye. The clock on the library wall ticked loudly, while Jack's mother, Lady Henley, seated in her chair by the fire, emitted gentle sobs from time to time from the depths of her handkerchief. Jack tried not to shift uncomfortably under his father's penetrating gaze. He dug the heels of his boots further into the Turkish carpet, but his hands were clutched tightly behind his back in a manner that belied his bold stance. It was an unpleasant moment for the handsome young man of twenty-six who had always basked in the glow of his parents' approval. For once, his youthful good looks, his fine, light brown hair, dancing blue eyes, and strong carriage did not help predispose his proud parent to be lenient with him. He fought the urge to hang his head.

"Well," prompted Sir Geoffrey finally, dropping the word like a stone into the silence. "What do you have to say for yourself?"

There was nothing that could be said to excuse him, Jack knew, but he continued to regard his father unflinchingly. "I can only give you my apologies, Father, and ask for your forgiveness." He swallowed, feeling an unfamiliar tightness beneath the knot of his cravat.

"Harrumph!" snorted Sir Geoffrey. Jack could tell the straightforward answer had not displeased his father, but Sir Geoffrey would never let that be known. "And I suppose I am to have your assurances that it will never happen again?"

Jack raised his chin higher and said, "I had better not venture to supply them, sir, for fear of disappointing you again."

Sir Geoffrey's eyes flashed in anger from beneath their grizzly brows. "If you think to impress me with your honesty, sir, you have missed your mark!" Jack winced. He had never known his father to be so beside himself with anger, especially not with his only son.

The baronet did not speak again until he had regained control of his temper. When he did, his words evoked a feeling of consternation in his listeners.

"I have no intention," he said firmly, "of allowing you to disappoint me again. As you so ably put it," he added with heavy irony.

"Sir?" said Jack, at a loss for his meaning. Lady Henley's sobs changed to a whimper.

Sir Geoffrey gave him a piercing glance, this time with so little pleasure in his expression that Jack had his first real moment of worry. "I have decided to pay your debts—all 20,000 pounds of them," he underscored. "But I do not intend to send you back to London so that you can waste your time and energy running up more."

He paused for a look at his son and then continued, speaking fiercely, "You know the pride I take in being the first Henley to bear the title baronet. Our family is an old and honoured one in this county, but it is entirely through my own efforts that we are in our present comfortable position!" He slapped his hand down suddenly on the top of his massive walnut desk.

Lady Henley's head jerked up quickly from her handkerchief as she uttered a startled, "Oh!"

Sir Geoffrey went on in a tone of regret, "With the start I had given you, Jack, I had hoped to see you, one day, made a peer. It is not part of my wish to watch you drink and gamble my fortune away before I hand it over to you and take my place underground!"

Jack's conscience, for the first time truly touched, prompted him to speak, but he was cut off before a word had left his lips.

"Enough!" said Sir Geoffrey, waving an impatient hand. "I do not want your reassurance! We have gone beyond the time for that. And after you hear what I have to say," he added wryly, "you may not be so anxious to comfort me." Jack forced his shoulders back and prepared to hear the worst.

Sir Geoffrey delivered his sentence in a quiet, but final tone, "I shall make you no further allowance as my heir."

Lady Henley gasped. Jack turned pale with surprise. He had not expected things to go this badly for him. He knew he had been extravagant and wild, but so were all his friends, and *they* eventually came about. What he had expected was for his father to insist upon a few months' rustication, or at most, a reduction in his allowance. But to cut off completely his only child and heir...

Jack looked at his father and saw that Sir Geoffrey was waiting for his reaction. He responded firmly, "Yes, sir."

"But Geoffrey!" protested Lady Henley tearfully. "Our poor boy will starve!"

"He is not a poor boy!" Sir Geoffrey retorted. "I hope to discover that he is a man. And, of course, he will not starve. He will do what many other men have done before him; he'll work for a living."

Jack swallowed again and his mind raced furiously. None knew better than he that he had not prepared himself for any gentlemanly career at university. Why should he when he was destined to inherit a comfortable baronetcy? Only younger sons were faced with the choice of church, army or navy, and Jack had given little thought to their plight except when one of his particular cronies had chosen such a path and could no longer share his amusements. His mother knew this as well as he.

"But Jack isn't fit to do anything, Geoffrey!" she said.

Her unhappy choice of words brought the two men's eyes together in amusement for the first time that day. Sir Geoffrey, glad to see the spark of humour still alive in his son despite his pronouncement, was softened.

"Nonsense, Maria," he said in a kinder tone. "Jack is as well able to care for himself as any man—better, I'll wager." Jack's brow rose in irony. Considering the announcement his father had just made, he found it less than comforting to hear such an expression of confidence. But Sir Geoffrey had not finished.

"I hope we shall learn that Jack is as suited to take my place ultimately as I believe him at heart to be." He paused and looked his son over once again. A glimmer of pride lit his eyes as he beheld his son's vigorous form.

"I do not intend to cast you off forever, Jack," he began again, "nor am I sending you out to find your own position. I realize, as you must, too, that you are not qualified for any of the nobler pursuits." He smiled to himself as he pictured his scapegrace son in a parson's surplice. "But you do have talents which can earn you sufficient income to keep you alive."

Sir Geoffrey glanced at his son once again before responding to Jack's puzzled look, this time with a trace of grim amusement in his expression. "I have secured a place for you as coachman on the London to Birmingham mail," he stated flatly.

Lady Henley gave a distressed cry. Jack started. Nothing could have been more unexpected. But before Jack could open his mouth to pose any questions, his mother began to wail.

"A coachman!" she cried in anguish. "A common coachman! Geoffrey, how could you? We shall all be disgraced!"

"It's quite all right, Mother," said Jack, amazed to find that his own spirits were rapidly recovering from the jolt. He went to her side and, putting an affectionate arm around her shoulders, presented her with his own lace-trimmed handkerchief. "I don't suppose anyone will have to know about it. It's not likely I'll run into any of your friends on the box, you know."

Lady Henley buried her face in the dry handkerchief and sobbed.

"That is quite enough now, Maria," said Sir Geoffrey gruffly, secretly ashamed to have caused her so much distress. "If Jack can take the news like a man, I see no reason for you to carry on in such a fashion. And it won't be forever, I assure you."

Jack looked up at this. His eyes held a question which caused Sir Geoffrey's confidence to falter for the first time. "I have no wish for my son to remain a coachman all his days," he said irritably, to hide his feelings. "As soon as Jack proves to me that he has mended his ways, and I am certain that he is worthy of my regard once again, I shall be happy to call him back into the family. But I cannot stand by and watch while he hastens to his ruin and takes the family honour with him. A good dose of hard work may be just the thing.

"And it strikes me as fitting that Jack should recoup some of the blunt he has undoubtedly thrown away on bribing the ostlers to secure him the box seat and the coachman to let him drive."

Jack suppressed his quick smile. "Touché," he acknowledged silently. Now that he understood his father's reasoning, Jack's feelings were considerably relieved. He could not question Sir Geoffrey's affection for him, and this alone had done much to remove the sting of his punishment. On the past few years, which he had spent in such idle pursuits as only London could offer, he was able to turn his back with no regrets. In truth, he realized, the amusements of Town, the gambling, the parties, and the drinking, had begun to pall. It was only now when he was presented with such a strange and entirely new challenge that he could understand their emptiness. He found that his heart was beating with an excitement he had never known.

Turning to his father with an open smile, he asked, "When and where am I to report?"

Sir Geoffrey looked at him and breathed an inner sigh of relief. His own belaboured spirits rose, too. "Tomorrow week," he said, "you will report to Mr. Waddell of the Castle Hotel in Birmingham." He stretched a hand to his only son, which was immediately seized and held. "You will not disappoint me this time," he said with a trace of hoarseness.

"I sincerely hope not, sir," said Jack, giving his father's hand a firm squeeze.

ONE WEEK LATER, Jack Henley, dressed in some serviceable breeches and a plain cotton shirt and waistcoat, for whose purchase he had been obliged to sell his gold fob, presented himself in the offices of the Birmingham mail. There he met with Mr. Waddell—stagecoach proprietor and mail contractor, and holder of the ancient and honourable office of Deputy Postmaster—who informed him of his weighty duties.

"Your ground," Mr. Waddell told him as they stepped outside to the yard, "will be from Oxford to Birmingham. That's over fifty miles. If you do it properly, I'll pay you ten shillings sixpence a week, but it is a long ground so you might reasonably expect to pick up another shilling from each passenger. But mind," he added sternly, stepping aside to allow a coach to clatter past him, "not one word beyond the first solicitation, even should you receive nothing by way of a courtesy. That's the absolute order of the General Post Office."

Jack promised to abide by this rule, wondering at the same time whether he would ever bring himself to ask for the first shilling. But Mr. Waddell was now pointing to a man who was descending from one of the coaches.

"And you must not expect to wear the G.P.O. livery," he continued, indicating the scarlet uniform in which the man was attired. "That's for the guard alone as representative of the Royal Mail. Some drivers are awarded it," he said fairly, "but only after years of faithful service. It's too early yet to be talking of that. You can be glad, at least, that the G.P.O. now sees fit to provide you with a uniform—it was not always the way. You'll have a hat, a coat of many capes, and a skin rug to warm your knees in case of bad weather. We'll take your measurements today and send them along to London."

Jack thanked him and hoped he sounded sufficiently grateful, but he must not have, for Mr. Waddell directed a serious look at him.

"I'll give you fair warning, young man," he said. "You'll be fined if your coach is late to any of its destinations, no matter what the cause. And I suggest you think twice before letting any of the passengers drive the coach, for you just might find yourself in a ditch with hell to pay. You've got a tough ground what with all the young gentlemen going up to university. And those young jackanapes will do anything for a lark. Well-breeched, most of 'em, and leaky as sieves when they climb on board. But just you mind the rules and you'll be all right."

Jack wondered if Mr. Waddell even suspected that Jack was one of the young jackanapes to whom he referred, for he had certainly done his share of bribing the ostlers. Once the seat on the box was gained, it was a fairly easy task to talk the driver into giving one the reins for a spell. But Jack had not realized, when he had done it, that he had been asking the coachmen to put their meagre incomes at risk. Just now, he was learning to have more respect for the simple comforts that income could provide.

But Mr. Waddell had not finished with him yet, having saved his most fearful warning for last. "I will caution you, too, not to shoulder any passengers whose names do not appear on the waybill in order to pocket their fares for yourself. The company has spies, and they will be quite ready to report you for the slightest infraction of the rules. And for this offence, if you are convicted, you might be transported for a period of seven years."

After this last bit of advice, Jack was glad that the dire warnings appeared to be at an end. Mr. Waddell turned from him and called to a squarely built man dressed in the scarlet livery, who came over to be introduced.

"This is Davies," Mr. Waddell said. "He'll be the guard assigned to you for most of your ground. Even though the coaches are the property of the contractors and not the Post Office, it's his job to see the coach arrives. He'll give the word to go, keep you to your speed and take action if there is a breakdown. He carries the timepiece in his shoulder pouch and will report the time at each stop along the road. That way, if you don't keep to your schedule, we'll know about it and can take the proper steps."

He clapped Jack on the back and added these final words: "Good luck to you, lad. You can count on Davies here. He'll keep you to your work."

Jack thanked Mr. Waddell and then examined the sober-looking fellow who was henceforth to be responsible for his conduct. He was relieved to find that Davies had an intelligent look about him, not like the sort of man who would fire his weapon for the pleasure of it, as so many were wont to do. Just now, he was giving Jack a careful scrutiny, too, so that Jack had an almost irrational desire to impress him favourably. He held out his hand in a friendly gesture, and Davies, after a moment's hesitation, took it.

"Don't look to me like a fellow what's used to hard work," was all he said.

Jack smiled and granted him the right of it, but added, "You needn't worry. I can handle the reins. And a fellow in my circumstances is happy to have the work." This answer seemed to satisfy the guard, for he simply nodded and got on with his duties.

JACK'S UNIFORM DULY ARRIVED and before long he was installed on a black-and-maroon coach, tastefully adorned with the royal arms and the four stars of the orders of knighthood and perched on wheels of Post Office red. The days that followed were long and hard, but they were not, as a rule, unpleasant. Starting at Oxford at 3:42 in the morning and arriving in Stratford upon Avon at 8:42, they were allowed twenty minutes to eat breakfast and see to the changing of the horses as well as to the passengers. The end of the day came just before noon, in time for dinner in Birmingham.

Happily, Jack found that he and the older guard worked well together. Davies proved to be as steady as he looked, and within a short time Jack could show him that his self-confidence on the box was more than just youthful boasting. At each stop along the way, a boy was certain to be sent from the inn with a mug full of brandy and water for the coachman, which Jack shared freely with his guard. If it were Davies and there happened to be no passenger on the roof that day, the guard would sometimes join him, abandoning his lonely seat on the rear of the coach for a bit of conversation. When his tongue was sufficiently loosened he would relate some of his experiences as guard on the mail, and Jack listened much amused. Jack was impressed as well with the guard's honesty. He never accepted mail to carry that was not duly registered with the coach's proprietors, though he might have made a considerable fee by contracting for it on his own.

Jack was never alone, for generally there was an adventurous young man or even a female passenger to sit the box beside him and pass the time. And he was fully occupied in keeping his horses to their demanding pace of nine miles an hour or better. It was not in Jack's character to sit the box like the lofty individuals who so often ruled that spot. He took a certain pleasure in seeing that his passengers were comfortably seated and their baggage settled for the journey. These gentlemanly attentions were so seldom seen on the road that, at first, the passengers reacted suspiciously to them. But eventually, Jack's friendly manner calmed their natural tendency towards wariness and engendered in them a feeling of confidence. Before long, Jack had earned the reputation of being a courteous, trustworthy driver, and the women passengers, in particular, were grateful for his solicitous care.

And all the while, Jack, whether he knew it or not, was undergoing a curious change. At first, he had cheerfully drained every mug of brandy and water that was brought to him, which helped to warm him against the weather. But he found himself so weary by the end of the day that when he arrived at his Birmingham lodgings, he tumbled right into his bed. And worse, the next morning it was all the more difficult to drag himself out of bed in the dark to have the new horses in harness by the time the coach arrived from London. Soon he accepted the offered spirits with more caution and found that his work became easier for his temperance.

Before long, too, he was faced with the problem of young gentlemen out of Oxford asking to be allowed to handle the reins. More often than not they were three sheets to the wind and would have landed Jack's coach in the ditch had they been given the chance. Jack's initial response had been to let them drive for a distance, as he had been allowed by many a coachman, but he was made uncomfortable by Davies's disapproval. And the resulting screams from the passengers, when the horses were sprung, had a sobering effect. Finally, on one particular occasion, when Jack was asked for the reins, his thoughts flew to that day's complement of passengers. There was an older woman who had given him a sweetly confiding smile upon mounting the steps, and a younger, nervous one with a newborn baby in her arms. So, on that occasion, Jack had smiled his winning smile and simply said no.

Three months were passed in this way without a major incident and Jack could be proud of his record. He was surprised to find that he did not miss the amusements of a gentleman's life, although there were days when a warm bath and the attentions of a valet would have been quite welcome. In fact, he settled rather quickly into the rhythm of his work and began to feel that there were advantages to being employed that he might never have realized if his father had not disowned him, however temporarily. From time to time he did wonder just when Sir Geoffrey would decide that he was worthy to be called his son again. But mail coachmen led a lordly life, after a fashion, for they were the kings of the road. All other traffic gave way for the mail, and it was the Royal Mail that carried the news of military victory to the provinces. All eyes would turn to see whether the coach carried the green laurels to signal another victory against Napoleon, and Jack was proud to be the herald of the Crown. He was not particularly eager to return to his old way of life.

It was in this happy frame of mind one morning at dawn that Jack pulled up in front of the inn in Shipston and espied a rather unusual customer.

CHAPTER TWO

SHE WAS CLEARLY A LADY, as he could tell by the elegance of her travelling costume, but she was unaccompanied by either governess or maid. She was small, with a slight, pleasant figure, cloaked in a cashmere wool redingote after the fashion of a few years back, and her curly, chestnut-coloured hair beneath a coal-scuttle bonnet was becomingly cut *à la Titus*. As Jack hopped down from the box to receive his passengers, she approached him, clutching her reticule anxiously.

"Are you the coachman on the London to Birmingham mail?" she asked.

"Yes, miss," replied Jack, bowing to her respectfully. "Are you meeting someone?"

"No." She flushed unexpectedly. "I tried to purchase a token, but the man in the booking office said there were no more places." She looked at Jack tentatively as though hoping he would prove the man wrong.

It went against his inclination to disappoint her, but he had to shake his head. "Then I'm sorry, miss. If the seats are all taken, you'll have to wait for the next coach or take the stage." Jack regretted his words as soon as he had said them, for her eyes, which had held a hopeful gleam, seemed suddenly to fade. There was something about the young lady, despite her small size, which suggested pluck, and it seemed to Jack that she was one who would face any problem head on. Her face gave the hint of a happy temperament and a lively intelligence, but at the moment there was a droop in her shoulders which did not belong there. She was evidently disheartened by his answer, although something told him disappointment was not new to her.

She received his answer calmly, though, and then gave him a measuring look before speaking again. He liked the clearness of her gaze.

In a voice barely above a whisper she asked, "Could you possibly find me a space upon the roof if I pay my passage? I will be happy to give you full fare."

Jack suppressed a smile at this inexpert attempt to bribe him. He had to admire her courage in pursuing the matter with him for he was for all intents and purposes a total stranger to her. What possibly could have happened to make her take a lone trip on the mail, he wondered, when she plainly looked to be a lady who would travel in her own coach or private chaise.

With the image of Davies's disapproving reaction in his mind, Jack started to tell her of the company's rule against allowing more than three passengers upon the roof, but as he opened his mouth to speak, something arrested him. The young lady was looking up at him hopefully, still clutching her reticule tightly with both hands. She was not desperate but he could tell something was disturbing her, and sufficiently so for her to need a faster means of travel than the stage offered. A cry from Davies alerted him to the fact that the coach was ready and he must hasten. He made a quick decision.

He winked at her and was gently amused by the moment's shock that registered in her face. Speaking loudly for the benefit of the other passengers, he said, "I'm quite sorry, miss, but this coach is full. You had better purchase a place in the next one."

She stared at him uncertainly as he said this, but then her face lit up as he added in a hurried whisper, "I can take you up beside me on the box, but not here in front of the booking office. If you'll give me your bags and walk up to the edge of town, I will take you up. I'll be there in less than two minutes."

Her eyes sparkled with sudden relief. "Thank you," she said in an answering whisper. "But you do not need to bother about my bags. They can follow me later."

With a quick smile, she turned and hastened up the street, leaving Jack to wonder how Davies would react to the presence of another passenger on the roof.

Once the coach was finally loaded with its full complement of passengers, Jack drove the horses down the few blocks to the end of town and drew them up. A young gentleman from Oxford had secured the box seat by paying a judicious tip to the horse handler. He looked at Jack questioningly as the horses stopped and the young lady stepped up to the wheel.

"Sorry, old fellow," Jack said to him, "But I must appeal to you as a gentleman to give up your seat to the lady. Her mother is ill and she must catch this mail to arrive at her side as quickly as possible."

The young man tipped his hat to the fair usurper, but spoke as one who must reluctantly point out the obvious. "I should be delighted, of course, but I feel I should mention the fact that all the seats on the roof are taken."

Jack looked behind him as if only now aware that such was the case. "I see, yes, you are quite right," he said musingly. "Yes, that does present a problem." He turned back to the gentleman and looked him over gravely. "Sir, may I trust you to ride on the rear of the roof near the guard? It is against postal regulations, as you know, but in this instance I think an exception could be made."

The young man assured him eagerly that he could be trusted, telling him that nothing would be further from his mind than robbing His Majesty's Mail, if only he might take one shot at a rabbit with the guard's blunderbuss. Hiding a smile, Jack told him with perfect untruth that he was certain Davies would be happy to oblige if he would only climb back and explain the situation to him.

The overjoyed passenger hastened to assume the forbidden seat at the back of the coach, despite the grumblings of the three on the roof as he climbed past them. Davies had been standing while this transaction took place, waiting patiently for Jack to resume the journey, though with a frown on his face. The young man spoke to him in a rapid undertone, and to Jack's relief, Davies merely gave him a quick, sardonic look before settling himself once again in the rear.

Hoping silently that his exemplary behaviour to date had purchased him the right to one transgression, Jack jumped down to help his gentle passenger up onto the box.

But the stopping of the coach had alerted the passengers inside to the fact that something was happening, and one woman in particular took offense at the sight of the lady waiting below. Sticking her red and pox-marked face out the window, she defied Jack to let "that creature" aboard.

The young lady glanced up at him worriedly and seemed, in the face of the woman's assault, to be questioning the wisdom of the step she was about to take. But her hesitation was only momentary. As soon as she perceived Jack's reassuring smile, she straightened her small shoulders and, accepting the use of his arm to help her mount, climbed to the wooden seat. Jack could see that she was unaccustomed to such abuse, and he admired her self-possession. Jack, however, had to answer to all of his passengers. So, suppressing a sigh of annoyance at the continuing torrent of slander emanating from the coach, he walked back to deal with the discontented woman.

"I shall have you reported to the authorities," she was threatening as he approached the door.

Jack smiled and addressed her with just the right degree of deference. "I would encourage you to do so, madam. It troubles me to offend you in such a manner, but there is only one solution as I can see it. I feel obliged to help the lady, who is on the way to her mother's deathbed and cannot find any means to get there quickly on her own. I would have asked one of you to relinquish your seat to her, but I did not wish to cause you any inconvenience."

The other passengers, startled by the thought that they might have been asked to give up their seats, retired willingly from the argument. The red-faced woman appeared slightly mollified, but she was not completely ready to abandon all appearance of offence.

"That's is as may be," she said in virtuous tones. "But how are we to know you'll keep your mind on the road—a young fellow like you, with a girl up beside him?"

Jack felt the justness of her remark as he recalled the lady's attractive appearance. It had been a long time, he reflected, since he had been in the company of a lady. But he did not reveal his feelings to the irate passenger. He merely bowed to the surprised woman with an exaggerated flourish.

"There, now, madam, you've discovered my reason for not asking *you* to sit on the box beside me," he said. The other passengers greeted this sally with hoots of laughter, and the red-faced woman turned an even deeper red. But she was not displeased to receive a compliment from such a handsome, well-spoken young man, so she waved Jack away with a muffled, "Go on," and many comments to her fellow passengers about his sauciness to a woman of her years.

Jack remounted the box and glanced quickly at his companion. He could tell by her heightened colour that she had heard his exchange with the other passengers and was trying to appear as if she had not. But Davies started to blow impatiently on his horn, so with no more than a respectful tip of his hat to the lady beside him, Jack took up the reins and started off once again.

From time to time he stole a look at his companion's profile. She was so small that her feet did not reach the footboard, and she was obliged to hold on tightly with both hands as Jack drove the coach rapidly around corners, trying to make up for the time he had lost. But soon they were out in the country and going at a more even pace where the road was straighter, and she could relax her hold a bit.

"I hope you will not have any cause to regret taking me up," she ventured after a while. "I shall only go as far as Hockley Heath, so you may let me down there. Shall I give you the fifteen shillings now?"

Jack grinned. "You might offer them to the young gentleman for giving up his seat to you," he said, jerking his head towards the rear of the coach. "But I think he is even better pleased to be riding illegally in the back than he was in front. And I make it a practice not to charge ladies who ride upon my box."

He could sense her start uncertainly at his answer. But he kept his gaze averted, and she must have been reassured by the serious tone of his voice for she answered him with composure, "Thank you."

They rode for a while in silence, but Jack found himself wishing she would speak to him again. He was very conscious of her skirt brushing against his leg, though she was seated as far from him as the wooden seat would allow. He was curious, too, about why she needed to travel so urgently, but his gentlemanly sensitivity would not have let him question her even if he had been dressed as Mr. Jack Henley. His present position was an even greater barrier to such a liberty.

Presently, he risked another glance in her direction. She was smiling in quiet satisfaction as she gazed about the countryside, and seemed completely free of that anxiety she had shown earlier. Whatever had caused her to flee in such haste now appeared to have been dismissed from her mind. The breeze was playing with the curls which peeked from beneath her bonnet and her eyes were bright with pleasure. Her small feet were swinging with each bounce of the coach, and they tapped against the wooden foreboot under his seat. Jack was happy to see that his initial assessment of her character had been correct. She was indeed a good-natured, gentle lady with a lively disposition and intelligence. He was happy to see the bright colour of pleasure and enthusiasm in her cheeks. Her carefree air awoke in him a strange elation.

Perhaps she sensed his eyes upon her, for she suddenly directed him a question.

"What is this coach called?" she asked. "Is it the Highflyer?"

"No, miss, that's a name for one of the stage-coaches," he said with a mixture of amusement and authority. "This is a patent coach, with a telegraph spring."

"It feels like a telegraph, it moves so quickly," she said. "With my feet dangling in the air and the smooth bounce it gives, I feel as if I'm flying. Your coach is very well sprung," she concluded approvingly. "I shall have to tell my grandfather."

Jack smothered a laugh. He knew she had intended the remark as a generous compliment. "Thank you, miss," he said gravely. "Is your grandfather a coaching gentleman?"

"Not any more," she answered with a hint of sadness. "But there was a time when he was quite good with the ribbons. He once raced from Maidenhead to Ascot in thirty-five minutes," she added proudly.

"That was excellent time," said Jack, forgetting to restrain his conversation in the face of her enthusiasm. "I doubt I could do it faster myself."

"Oh, grandpapa had quite a reputation," she said. "He was an active member of the Benson Driving Club until quite recently. He used to take me up beside him on the box when I was just a baby, though my mother tried to stop him."

Seeing her obvious pleasure and enjoyment of the adventure, Jack thought her childhood experience would likely explain her current air of ease on the jolting box. He found it easy to picture her as a little girl holding on tightly and laughing with delight.

"Any man would be proud to have you sitting up beside him," he said without thinking, "with your pretty curls peeking out from beneath your bonnet."

The young lady stared at him in sudden dismay, and Jack's heart sank as he realized what he had done. She turned from him, but not before he saw the gentle reproach in her eyes. His own face coloured in vexation as he turned, too, to stare at the road.

Jack cursed himself silently. How could he have been so stupid! The remark itself had not been so offensive. It was certainly no more—probably less—flirtatious than anything he might have said to a lady friend in London under comparable circumstances. But this lady clearly thought she had been insulted by a servant of the Birmingham mail! And why shouldn't she, he reflected, for who else would be driving a coach full of passengers?

He clenched his jaw firmly and unconsciously tightened his grip upon the reins. For the first time these three months, Jack realized that his father had indeed imposed a punishment when he had sent him to work for the mail. His mind wandered as he thought about whether he ought to apologize to the young lady or just allow the matter to drop. He considered telling her about his own circumstances by way of explanation for his forwardness, but it occurred to him that she might very well not believe him. His hands tightened even more on the reins.

Jack was so preoccupied that he did not notice that the horses were beginning to object to this unaccustomed treatment, tossing their heads in an attempt to loosen the hold upon them. As if aware of his own tension, they began to pick up their pace.

Suddenly, one of the leaders tripped, pulling sharply upon the rein, which must have been worn in one spot, for it broke in two with a sudden snap. Instantly, the unguided and frightened horse began to run and the carriage was propelled with a powerful jerk. The other leader became alarmed and, bound to the frightened horse by its coupling reins, attempted to follow, but it was held in check by the pressure of Jack's hold on the reins. This uneven situation caused the coach to sway back and forth as the loosened lead horse kept trying to escape his traces. Jack was pulling on the reins which were still intact and fighting to regain control of the frightened animals, but his companion, with no foothold to support her, was being tossed dangerously to the left and right. Suddenly, her grip broke and she was thrown abruptly against Jack's side.

He quickly let loose of the reins and caught her with one arm before she could be flung from the box, but with his hold firmly about her waist he could not manage to regain his grip. The reins for the right pair of horses were flapping beyond his reach. There was nothing he could do but hold on with his left hand with all his strength as the horses plunged wildly down the road. The brake stood at his side, but without a free hand Jack was helpless to avail himself of it. The muscles of his left arm were straining against the weight of the horses, and he called to them to hold up, while the passengers' screams of dismay were filling his ears.

Finally, just as Jack was certain he could not hold on much longer, the horses grew weary and began to slow. He called to them reassuringly and his words took effect, so that even though the coach still swayed with the uneven stopping of the loose horse versus the others, he eventually managed to bring it to a halt near a grove of oak trees.

Slowly releasing his aching fingers from the leather straps, he sighed with relief and, closing his eyes, leaned against the hard back of the seat. It was only then he became aware that he was still gripping his tiny passenger firmly by the waist. He had been holding her so tightly, and she was so small, that she was now practically sitting on his lap. She sat astride his right leg, her feet dangling down about his ankles. Abruptly, as if just realizing her awkward position herself, she placed her hands upon his arm and pushed it away, while she quietly struggled to resume her place.

Giving her his hand to help her back onto her seat, Jack swallowed with chagrin, and another, peculiar emotion, which made his heart beat strangely when she turned her embarrassed eyes to him in a quick glance.

"I hope you weren't injured in any way, miss," said Jack humbly, his voice coming hoarsely. He meant to avert his gaze, but for some inexplicable reason found it impossible to do so. The young lady, however, had recovered more quickly, for even though her embarrassment was still perceptible, she managed to incline her head in a condescendingly correct manner.

"No," she answered. "Thank you. I was not. But I must commend you," she added, turning away from him briskly and resuming her erect posture, "for your able handling of the situation."

Jack thanked her and leaned back against the rear of the seat once again, allowing himself one moment before descending to deal with his duties. His left arm was aching terribly and he sighed with dismay as he contemplated the hours of repair that were surely before him. It would be a severe penance for the few seconds' pleasure of holding his companion about the waist. The passengers were moaning in protest and a few of the women were weeping. He could not ignore them. Slowly and painfully, then, he descended from the box.

Davies and the other young gentleman, who had rather miraculously managed to hold on during the wild careening of the coach, had already sprung down and were doing their best to calm the ladies. Jack threw them a grateful look and went first to secure the horses. He already knew what the problem was and saw nothing for it but to lead the horses into the next village and wait for new harness to be provided. The passengers, he knew, would not be happy to have to wait, and it was possible that word of his own carelessness might get back to the proprietors, and that his pay would be severely docked. The threat of transportation arose in his mind.

The horses were surprisingly calm after their rash performance. Jack knew that they were merely exhausted and too much so to fly off the handle again.

He secured both leaders to a tree and allowed them to cool off, while he returned to face the passengers. It would be up to Davies to ride one of the leaders to the next stop to get the mail forward.

Although Davies's calm logic had done much to restore the goodwill of those inside the carriage, when Jack stepped up he was greeted by a chorus of complaints.

"I knew no good would come of letting that girl up on the box!" asserted the red-faced woman amidst the others' comments.

Acutely aware of his own inattention for that very reason, Jack was hard-pressed to answer her courteously, but he spoke with admirable restraint. "You are mistaken, madam. A rein on one of the leaders has simply broken and I cannot imagine how a passenger on the box could be considered responsible. It happens from time to time. I am sorry the horses bolted and caused you such discomfort, but I assure you the matter will be dealt with as soon as possible."

His calm, polite manner had its usual effect, for even though a murmur greeted his words, it was largely in favour of the justness of his remarks. Taking this as a sign that he might now get on with the unpleasant task of walking the horses to the next village, Jack went back to unharness them.

Davies climbed back up to his seat to unlock the box which held the mail. But, as Jack approached the front of the carriage with the intention of offering to help his mysterious passenger down from the box, that young lady hailed him.

"Pardon me," she said quite eagerly and without a trace of her earlier embarrassment, "but I think I might be of some assistance."

Jack smiled openly at the thought of such a slight girl helping him with his wearisome task and offered his hand to help her alight. "Could you, miss?" he asked indulgently.

"Oh, yes, I'm almost certain," she said, beginning to fumble in her reticule. Jack watched her with undisguised delight, thinking it was almost worth having had the accident to see what she would produce from it. In a moment, she had pulled a strange object from her bag and was holding it up triumphantly for his inspection.

"There! You see?" she said.

Jack reached out and took the small object. It was a contraption of sorts, made of a short length of leather harness with two buckles, one on each end. As he examined it, Jack began to feel that perhaps it could be of some use to him. He looked up at his passenger, his curiosity fully aroused.

"What is it, if you please? How does it work?"

The lady took back the contraption and walked over to the horses with Jack half a step behind.

"I will show you," she said. "You see, you must simply cut a hole in each end of the broken strap and then thread each of them through a buckle—like this." She showed him how the two ends fit into the buckles, and Jack could see that the contraption would indeed provide a temporary solution to his problem.

"I don't suppose you should go very far without having the harness repaired," she concluded, "for it wasn't meant to do more than help one on to the next stop. But it ought to do as far as that."

"That far and then some," agreed Jack. "What a clever device! How did you come by it?"

"My grandfather made it," she said proudly. "He copied it from a friend's invention. And he has always insisted that I carry it with me whenever I travel."

"It's a stroke of genius!" declared Jack. "I will set to work on those holes right away." He handed the buckles back to her, and, taking a knife, began to cut small holes through the broken pieces of strap. The young lady stood waiting without complaint and even seemed pleased to be assisting in such an important task.

When he had finished, Jack reached out and took the buckles from her hand. "I must confess," he said smiling, "that I did not see what you could possibly have in that reticule to assist me."

She laughed. "I suppose not. And I will confess that this is the first time I have had cause to use it. I have transferred it from one bag to the next many times, wondering if I were just being foolish. But I could not bring myself not to carry it when my grandfather trusted me to do so. I have almost become superstitious about it."

"Well, it certainly proved useful today," Jack said. "You have my sincere gratitude." He smiled and almost extended a hand before recollecting himself.

The young lady must have detected the aborted gesture, however, for she coloured slightly and looked away. "I was most happy to be of service," she said, inclining her head gracefully.

Jack was once again abashed, but this time it was not for his impertinence. He knew that his lovely passenger had not intended to reprove him for what was no more than a friendly gesture. But he was angry with himself for forgetting his subservient position. The truth of the matter was, he thought, that he was having such fun talking to this unnamed lady that he could not remember to keep his mind on his job.

Resolutely he turned back to work. Davies came hurrying up with the mail bag, but Jack showed him the young lady's device which would allow him to fix the reins in a trice. The older man grunted with satisfaction, and, after giving a respectful tip of his hat to Jack's companion, returned the mail to its box in the boot. In a moment they were ready to proceed. Jack handed the young lady back up onto the box and informed the rest of the passengers of their good luck. Even the red-faced woman was happy to hear that they would not be obliged to wait untold hours for the horses to be brought back to the coach, and Davies looked on with grateful relief.

So Jack was able to resume his seat with the satisfaction that all was well and the impossible had been accomplished in a matter of minutes. Hardly any time had been lost, for the horses had bolted in the right direction and their run had almost offset the time the coach had been stationary. Still, Jack knew he must be careful not to risk straining the horses further, so he kept them to an even pace for the remainder of that leg of the journey.

He was glad to find that his improper degree of friendliness had not silenced his companion completely, for as soon as they started off again, she began to chat as easily as before. This time Jack was careful not to forget himself and they passed the rest of the trip happily. The young lady expressed such an interest in his driving that he would have liked to offer her the chance to handle the ribbons, but he feared such an offer might throw her out of countenance. As small as she was, he would have to have maintained his own hold on the reins, and that would not have done.

In spite of the slow pace of the horses, it seemed to Jack that they arrived in Hockley Heath all too soon and his pretty passenger prepared to alight.

"I could return your grandfather's contraption to you on my way back through town," he suggested, not without a flicker of hope, as they threaded their way through the village.

The young lady seemed to withdraw slightly, as though she feared an assumption of familiarity on his part. But she gave him a polite smile. "That will not be necessary," she said. "I do not mean to travel again soon, but were I to do so, I am certain my grandfather would have another he could give me."

Jack tried to sound as if he had no other interest in the matter, but it cost him no small effort. "That's all right, then. But I must thank you again for coming to my assistance."

She inclined her head, and dimpled slightly. "It will please my grandfather enormously to know I finally had use for it."

Jack laughed. "I'm certain it will." Reluctantly then, he drew the horses to a stop before they came to the inn where they were to be changed. "Is this the place you wish to be set down?"

"Yes, this will be just right," she said. He thought he detected a slight sigh, but she did not meet his eye.

He jumped down off the box and helped her to climb down. Then he stood uneasily, wishing to take her hand but knowing it could not be offered.

"Goodbye, miss," he said, hoping his voice did not betray his reluctance to see her go.

"Goodbye—and thank you for taking me up," she replied with only a slight hesitation. Then she walked away, but not without giving him a gentle smile. He watched her for a moment until Davies called out to remind him of the time. Then he turned back to the coach, his expression grim.

The change of horses and harness was accomplished in two minutes and Jack hastened the coach onwards for the last leg of his ground, hoping to arrive in Birmingham on time despite the accident. Before they were far out of the village, Davies climbed forward and joined him on the box. He looked at Jack with a curious glint in his eye.

"An agreeable young lady," he observed as Jack stared at the road in front of him. "Not a bit high in the instep, as anybody can see she'd a right to be."

"Yes, she was and no, she wasn't," answered Jack, but not in a tone to invite more comment.

"Saved your hide, she did," the guard then said, winning a reluctant chuckle from Jack. "I'll have to report the incident on the time bill next stop, but I don't think I'll need to mention her in my final report. The contractor back in Shipston gave us a faulty set of harness, that's all, and the coachman patched the harness so we could proceed." Jack threw him a grateful smile, but was soon staring ahead again, lost in thought.

Davies smiled enigmatically and then turned to gaze at the horses. His companion was silent for the rest of the journey and there was a grim, almost brooding air about him. Anyone might have said, looking at him, that there was a young man who was no longer content with the hand that had been dealt to him. And on this particular day, they would have been right.

CHAPTER THREE

THE HONOURABLE Cecily Wolverton (for that was his passenger's name) strolled briskly into the inn in search of a gig to borrow. She was greeted by the innkeeper with much consternation.

"You may borrow my gig, Miss Cecily, and welcome you are to it, but I will not be having you drive up to your grandfather's house with no female to companion you. I don't know what the world's coming to, but what I do know is your grandfather would rip up at me something fierce if you was to show up at the manor in my gig with no maid. I'll tell Betsy to go along with you and our Henry will be up there in no time to fetch the gig back."

Cecily thought it best not to protest, for she knew the innkeeper to be right about her grandfather's opinion of the matter. So she resolved to tip Henry handsomely for his trouble. The gig was soon brought round, and Cecily set off on the three-mile drive to her grandfather's house with her hands on the reins and Betsy at her side.

When she drew up before the manor, the door opened and more voices were added to the innkeeper's, predicting dire consequences to her morning escapade. Sir Waldo Staveley was a just master, but there was nothing in his behaviour to suggest that he would condone the arrival of his granddaughter in anything less than his own chaise. Mrs. Selby, Sir Waldo's housekeeper, was almost beside herself with injury.

"I will take you to your rooms, Miss Cecily, not but what they aren't ready for you, as they would have been if you had waited for your grandfather's chaise he was sending in nobbut two days. And I will have your bags taken up. But it'll have to be Selby what tells him you've come in such a hamper-skamper fashion for I'm sure I wouldn't dare to do so."

"I have no bags for the present," answered Cecily sympathetically, "and I am so sorry for throwing you off keel like this, Mrs. Selby. But I had to do it, and that's that. If Selby will be so kind as simply to announce me to my grandfather, I shall explain my irregular behaviour to him myself, and I am certain all will be right."

"No bags!" exclaimed Mrs. Selby, more offended by this, it seemed, than by anything else. "I don't know what things is coming to, Miss Cecily, I really don't. But," she added more kindly, seeing a sudden tired look on her mistress's pretty, young face, "you will want to tidy up now and have a bit of rest. Those mail coaches go so fast, it's a wonder you arrived in one piece, and you'll likely be done up with all the bouncing and rocking. I'll have Selby announce you after you've rested and are ready to see your grandfather."

Cecily smiled at her gratefully and did take a minute to lie down upon the bed. The journey had been filled with stressful events, not the least of which had been her reason for making it. But right now she gave little thought to the cause of her flight. Her eyes closed and she immediately saw the face of the young coachman as he had looked when gazing at her so admiringly. She shook her head, but the vision persisted. He had been totally unlike what she would have expected a mail coachman to be, she thought. Young, handsome, well-spoken and clean, he might have been a much higher class of person. In fact, she thought, if she had met him under different circumstances and in different garb, she might have taken him for an equal!

Cecily sighed. It was a pity that none of the gentlemen she had met were so handsome and personable—not that any of them would be interested in her in her present circumstances if they were. Only three years ago, she had been an heiress of such standing as to be an eligible bride for a nobleman of the highest rank. The only child of the Baron and Baroness of Stourport, Cecily was to inherit the major part of the Stourport estate, which had come into her family through her mother.

Her maternal grandfather, the first Lord Stourport, had been granted the barony for extraordinary military service to the Crown. Because the baron had no sons, the patent of creation had specified Cecily's mother as his successor in order that the title might pass to his direct line, with remainder to heirs general. Cecily's father, Mr. Stephen Staveley, had assumed his wife's patronymic, Wolverton, by Royal licence. They had had no sons. But during their lifetimes, Cecily's parents had built a considerable estate which, due to the unusual origin of their titles, need not have formed part of the barony. Cecily, had she inherited, could have had every expectation of becoming a peeress in her own right, as had her mother.

But two years ago, upon her father's death, no will had been found. His solicitor had confirmed the fact that a will had been drawn up in Cecily's favour and signed, but Lord Stourport had not trusted solicitors and had kept the will at home. An exhaustive search had turned up nothing; the estate had entered the probate courts; and after lengthy legal battles the court had decided the laws of primogeniture should be followed. The Stourport estate, along with the barony, had passed to Cecily's Cousin Alfred, and Cecily had taken up residence with her Aunt Emma.

Alfred. At the thought of him, Cecily frowned with vexation. If it had not been for Alfred she would not have fled her aunt's house so rashly. She did not regret her departure, for the day had proven to be singularly interesting, but she feared this would not be the last day to be shadowed by Alfred. She had been planning to move into her grandfather's house, and his carriage was to have been sent for her two days hence. But yesterday she had received a note from Alfred which had made it imperative for her to undertake the journey on her own.

The thought of Alfred's note was enough to make her livid. The little beast had had the nerve to send her a most offensive letter, although it was couched in the most respectful tone, as were all Alfred's speeches even when what he said was intended to reduce one to ashes. But its suggestion was so offensive, so odious! Alfred had not taken any pains to remain part of Cecily's life after the court judgement, although he had expressed his regrets for the part he had to play in the loss of her estate. Cecily had never quite believed that his regrets were sincere—but now! If anyone else had penned that note to her, she would have had to consider it a romantic overture! But knowing him as she did, she could not believe Afred had the slightest interest in her womanly charms.

She rose to her feet with a sigh and, after freshening herself, went to visit her grandfather. Sir Waldo was now confined to his bed, his gout and rheumatism having crippled him. Cecily tapped softly at the door and heard a gruff, "Come in."

She tiptoed up to the bed and planted a kiss on her grandfather's cheek, but was not greeted with his usual chuckle.

"Do not think to wheedle me out of my anger, Miss Cecy, for I tell you it will not do!" said Sir Waldo.

"Of course, it will not," agreed Cecily. "I should never have imposed on you in such a way."

Sir Waldo blustered for a moment and then said, "Nonsense, girl. You're trying to come over me with your tricks. You know very well I'm glad to see you. Why, I've been trying to get you to come live with me, haven't I? It's not that and you know it!"

"I know, Grandpapa," said Cecily, placing her cheek against his forehead. "Nobody loves me more or cares for me better than you." An involuntary tear rose in her eye and was quickly wiped away.

"There, there now," said Sir Waldo, becoming alarmed and giving her a few rapid pats on the hand. "There's no need to cry. I'm not angry with you. I only want to know what possessed your Aunt Emma to let a girl your age travel alone—and on the mail! She must have lost her faculties, or did you wheedle her, too?"

"No, I didn't wheedle her," said Cecily, smiling at his favourite word where she was concerned. "But I simply had to leave at once, and there was no other choice. My aunt did not like it, but I made her see it must be done."

Sir Waldo's brow wrinkled into a worried frown. "What's happened now, puss?"

Cecily tried to make light of it. "You'll say it wasn't much," she said, laughing, "but I can tell you it mattered to me. I had to get away from the Odious Alfred!"

"That loose screw!" cried Sir Waldo, getting all red in the face. "What's he doing bothering you? I should think he'd done enough damage, cheating you out of your fortune."

"It's all right," said Cecily calmly, placing a cool hand on his brow. "You mustn't let it excite you. I'm here now, and none the worse. It was simply that Alfred wrote me a note, advising me of his intention to call on the morrow, and the only way I could see to avoid him was to hop aboard the mail and come straight to you. That way, Aunt Emma can say that I've gone on a visit and missed his letter entirely."

Sir Waldo looked at her anxiously. "A call? Since when does that hedgebird pay you calls? He don't plan to make you an allowance, I suppose?"

Cecily shook her head. "I can't believe he would," she said, "not after all this time has passed." Then she added quite sincerely, "I really don't know what Alfred's intentions are."

"Hummph!" snorted Sir Waldo. "I don't suppose you would. No decent person could understand that . . . that . . ." Here Sir Waldo's vocabulary failed him.

"No," agreed Cecily, amused by seeing her grandfather at a loss for words. "I don't suppose they would."

She waited until Sir Waldo was calmer, planning to divert him with her account of the coach ride, but a sudden notion struck him.

"Cecily," he said, his hands shaking slightly in hers. "I know you don't care to speak of it, but you don't suppose that Alfred—that he somehow has managed to find your father's will?"

Cecily looked at him for a startled moment. "I suppose it's possible," she said. Then, giving her head a slight shake, she added, "But surely if he had found the will he would have notified my father's solicitors and they would have contacted me directly. If I know Alfred, he would want to make certain of its being verified before handing the property over to me. He would not be so anxious to part with it."

Sir Waldo snorted. "If he's the man I think him, he would destroy any document he came across. Not like him to fork over the dibs once he'd got his hands on it. No, that cannot be the reason. Don't know what got into me to suggest such a thing. Oughtn't to have mentioned it."

He looked so down at the mouth, that Cecily hurried to comfort him.

"That's quite all right, Grandpapa. You cannot help wishing for the impossible any more than I can. Papa made no secret of his intentions to bequeath the property to me. What I cannot bear is the thought that he might have changed his mind for some unfathomable reason."

"That he wouldn't have!" asserted Sir Waldo firmly. "I know Stephen could be peculiar when he chose. I'll never know what possessed him not to leave the will with his solicitors; he could be more crochety that I am about some matters. But I *do* know he meant to leave the property to you, and no one shall ever persuade me to change my mind about that!"

"I know," said Cecily gratefully. "But what's done is done, and there's nothing more to say."

"Perhaps not," said her grandfather, frowning at his own helplessness. "But I have thought and thought about it, lying here—without being able to come up with the answer. I would give my front teeth to know what became of that will!"

"So would I," agreed Cecily seriously, in spite of the peculiar image this conjured up. "But," she said with forced cheeriness, "since Alfred has never invited me back to Stourport so I might tap the walls looking for hiding places, I don't suppose we were meant to know. Let's not talk about this any more, shall we? Let me tell you about my trip today."

Sir Waldo patted her hand indulgently. "There's a puss," he said. "All right, tell me about your ride."

"Well," she said giving him a saucy look. "I rode upon the box."

"You what?"

"I rode upon the box," she confirmed.

"You mean to say," he said, lowering his brows threateningly, "that the proprietors had no more sense than to risk your life on the box?"

"As you did so many times?" she reminded him. "No, it wasn't their fault. The coach was booked, but the coachman allowed one of the passengers to ride next to the guard and took me up beside him."

"And charged you a pretty penny for the privilege, too, I'll warrant," said Sir Waldo, outraged.

"As a matter of fact, he didn't charge me at all," Cecily told him.

Sir Waldo's brows rose in surprise. "A peculiar sort of coachman, that, if you ask me."

Cecily flushed unexpectedly. "Yes, he was," she confessed. "He was quite well-spoken and most polite. I had not expected to find such good manners in a coachman."

This information seemed to please her grandfather. "Well," he said, "I fancy it is due to the interest of gentlemen such as myself that we begin to see improvements in the men's manners. It is a matter of pride to the members of the Benson Driving Club that our patronage has done much to bring about a change for the better. A little recognition, a kind word and a good meal, a consultation on the finer points of driving—all these things help to show our servants of the road that they are valued for the excellent job they do. And in return they please us by improving their manners—watching their language before the passengers and so on." He chuckled indulgently. "Of course, they are often puffed up with their own consequence, but we mustn't deny them their pride."

Cecily started to protest. Her coachman had not seemed conceited in the least. Of course, he had been a bit above himself at times—he really did not seem to remember his station. But she could not call it conceit. He simply seemed unaware from time time of the distinction between them, so much so that she had almost forgotten it herself! Perhaps it was due to a peculiar upbringing he may have had. Nevertheless, she did not bother to protest her grandfather's reading of the coachman's character. It did not really matter, after all, and it would be most particular of her to point it out.

Instead, she told him about the reins breaking and how his leather contraption had saved the day. She did not tell him, of course, that she had been dangerously flung about, nor that the coachman had been forced to take certain liberties to save her. Sir Waldo was highly gratified by the story and Cecily was happy to see that his good humour was completely restored. Sometimes she feared that another blow such as the loss of her estate would be more than her ailing grandfather could stand, and she hoped never to have to alarm him with further news of Alfred's perfidy.

She stayed with him for a while longer, personally tending to the little details of his comfort, which she knew pleased him. Then she made arrangements for her bags to be fetched and brought to the manor as soon as possible, and ordered a small meal to be brought to her room.

It was taken up by Mrs. Selby herself, who returned to the kitchen some time later in a most disagreeable frame of mind. She was so irritable with her husband for the remainder of the day that he finally begged to be told the reason for her rare taking.

"It's Miss Cecily," she finally admitted. "I don't care to see her so mopish as she's been. Oh, she tries to hide it!" she added. "But I who knows her can see that she's still cut up about her father's will. And it's not right for a pretty young thing like her to be shut away with an old man when she ought to be out dancing and having a merry time."

Mr. Selby, taking offense at the implied criticism of Sir Waldo, began to protest, but she cut him off.

"You don't have to go telling me that it's not the master's fault, Mr. Selby. Nobody knows that more than me. Why, where else should she be but with her grandfather who loves her! But what she's going to do when he moves on, I don't know."

Mr. Selby made bold to speak again. "As I informed you in confidence, Mrs. Selby, having received the knowledge of it from Sir Waldo himself, the master has made provision for her in his will to the best of his ability."

She scoffed. "Two thousand pounds! When she expected to inherit that much income a year! I know he's done his best for her, but you can't expect it'll make up to her for all she's lost!"

Her husband responded primly. "There will be plenty of young gentlemen who will not scorn to ally themselves with woman possessed of a fortune that size."

"I would not be so certain, Mr. Selby," his wife objected. "It may seem like a fortune to you or me, but it's not what she's used to. And if there *are* so many young gentlemen, where are they? I used to worry she might be chased by some fortune hunter and not know the difference, but there's not much chance of that now. When you thinks he was all set to go to London to have her come-out before the scandal and then had to settle for Stratford upon Avon instead! She couldn't be squandering her little bit of fortune on London then, could she? And the rumours that was flying! I know. Her aunt Emma's housekeeper, that Mrs. Green that used to live in Hockley Heath before she married, she told me what they was saying. Calling my pretty 'poor Miss Cecily' and the like. Her relatives and their servants, too—treating her like a poor relation—when she was used to being treated like a princess! It stood to reason with all the money she was supposed to get. But it never turned her head. Not at all." Mrs. Selby sighed.

Her husband and workmate of the past forty years tried to quiet her fears then, but it was no use. She refused to be comforted.

"It's no wonder she's come to us," she told him. "Us who loves her. Her aunt Emma means well, but it's them others. They're not likely to let her forget she's living on their charity now, are they? And when she's not got Sir Waldo...to think of her living on her own without nobbut two thousand pounds between her and the poorhouse, having to eke out her income in dismal lodgings somewhere with nobody but the parson for society! It's more than I can bear to think on, Mr. Selby!" And she shocked her proper husband suddenly by bursting into tears.

MEANWHILE, CECILY, lying on her bed, was speculating on how her coachman would look in buckskin trousers and a coat of blue superfine. His strong chest would certainly fill it nicely and she had no doubt his legs would look admirably in the skintight trousers.

She shook herself abruptly. What had been thinking of! A coachman, indeed! If the temptations of the flesh were as great as she had often heard they were, she could see why mésalliances were so often formed. But she trusted she would never descend to a level of such desperation that she would encourage a common coachman to make love to her. She'd as lief run off with the footman! At least then she could expect to find employment under the same roof as her husband. But what would a coachman's wife do? When would he be home? And what would be the good of having such a handsome young husband if he were always from home?

She laughed out loud. No doubt it was the jolting of the coach which had addled her brains. Mrs. Selby was right: taking a seat on the mail was no safe way for a lady to travel.

CHAPTER FOUR

ONE MORNING, about a month later, Cecily was engaged in a thorough cleaning of her grandfather's library, when Mrs. Selby interrupted her with some news.

The library at the manor had been neglected for some time. Sir Waldo was not a serious scholar, though he did have his favourites among the classics, which were those works given to the sporting inclinations of the Greeks and Romans. The remainder of his collection lay ignored, and it was into these books Cecily had decided to sail, armed with a feather duster. Her hair was confined in an old cap and her clothes had gathered more dust than her trusty implement. She wiped her hands on her apron as Mrs. Selby made her announcement.

"Word's come up from the inn at Hockley Heath, Miss Cecily. There's a coachman been injured. Broke his leg, he did, when the axle broke and he got tossed off the box. Mr. Rose, down at the inn, thought you'd better be told about it, seeing as how Sir Waldo might want to know."

Cecily stepped down off the stool she had been using and reached up to untie her cap. "Yes, thank you, Mrs. Selby. I am certain Sir Waldo would want him carried up to the manor. You may send word to Mr. Rose, with my grandfather's compliments, that the poor fellow will be welcome here as soon as he is able to be moved. And please make certain the doctor has been sent for. Sir Waldo will take care of everything. I know Mr. Rose will not like to have one of his rooms taken up for whatever time the man shall be needing to convalesce."

"Yes, miss," said Mrs. Selby gloomily. She did not relish the thought of caring for an outsider for the next six weeks or more. But it was no use arguing, for Sir Waldo would be outraged if he thought a fellow man of the road had not been properly cared for. She left the room and Cecily, not loath to conclude her work, prepared to carry the news to her grandfather.

She stopped by her own room and freshened up before presenting herself. He would not like to think she had been engaged upon such a menial task as dusting, but the truth was she was bored. Only by keeping herself busy with the housekeeping was she able to conquer a certain staleness in her days. And Mrs. Selby, beginning to age herself, was not ungrateful for the assistance.

After putting on a fresh gown and washing up to the elbows, Cecily tripped along to her grandfather's bedroom and scratched at the door.

"Come in! Come in!" answered Sir Waldo testily. Cecily suppressed a smile and entered, only to find him scowling at the coverlets.

"So there you are, girl!" he said accusingly. "I thought you might have gone off to your aunt's visiting and forgot to tell me goodbye. What have you been doing with yourself?"

"Oh, Grandpapa!" protested Cecily. "As if I would leave you and not say a word! Did I not carry up your tea myself this morning? Or have you forgotten already?"

Sir Waldo was abashed. "No, I have not forgotten, Cecy. You mustn't take any notice of what I say. It's just that I haven't anything to do or think about in this confounded bed. I might just as well be underground."

"Nonsense," said Cecily calmly. They had had this conversation before, and she knew his mood would soon change. She began to tuck the covers more tightly around the mattress and offered him her news.

"I have something to tell you which should cheer you considerably, Grandpapa. There's been a coachman injured in the village and they will be bringing him up to the manor shortly. I have already given the instructions."

"Harrumph!" growled Sir Waldo. "A pretty fellow you must think me if you suppose I would be cheered by some poor boy's breaking his neck!"

Cecily laughed and the old man was forced to hide a smile. "It is not his neck. You know very well that is not what I meant, you sly old thing," she protested. "He has broken his leg, however, and will need a bed for several weeks. I thought you might like to have a chat or two with him when he's better."

Sir Waldo's frown had lifted and he did seem cheered as he took out his watch. "Must have been the mail coachman," he said musingly. "Could even be the fellow who took you up."

Cecily's hands stilled and she flushed inexplicably. Then she resumed smoothing the coverlets, saying briskly, "Well, I shall be sorry if it is. I would not wish an accident on such a pleasant man. But quite likely it is someone else. After all, it has been more than a month, surely."

"Has it?" asked Sir Waldo absently.

Cecily could tell that he was already thinking ahead to the prospective chat with the coachman. She was glad to see the spark of interest on her grandfather's face, and grateful for the stimulus in spite of the injury to the poor driver. If she was bored with all she had to occupy her, how much worse must it be for her grandfather, who had led such an active life, to be confined now to his bed. She stayed with him and talked until his servant came to give him his luncheon.

Another hour later, Cecily was finishing her own meal when the sound of a bustle in the servants' hall signalled the arrival of the injured man. Chiding herself for a sudden feeling of nervousness, Cecily rose from the dining table and went to make certain that everything possible was being done for him. Sir Waldo had given her strict instructions to see that the poor man was well treated, and he expected her to report back to him that evening.

As Cecily entered the hall, her ears were greeted by a rather familiar voice raised in cheer.

"That's right, gentlemen, just place me here, over by the fire. I'm certain Cook and I shall get along famously. I can tell by the smell that she's a person of extraordinary talent." And then, "Oops! Not that leg, my good man. It's already had its share of troubles today. And I'd as lief keep it as the other one, thank you!"

Cecily covered her mouth so as not to laugh at the coachman's brazenness. It was certainly *her* coachman, she reflected, and still not remembering to keep to his own station, by the sound of him. She realized at once that the innkeeper must have supplied him generously with spirits while they waited for the doctor to arrive, and she supposed he was enjoying all the fuss being made over him.

But it would not do for him to disrupt her grandfather's household. So, stepping up to the group of people surrounding his pallet, she spoke with a sternness she did not feel. "What is the meaning of this, pray? Is there anything amiss?"

The servants turned to regard her with consternation. Doctor Whiting and Mr. Rose, the innkeeper, were standing among them.

"Begging your pardon, Miss Cecily," said Mr. Rose, "but I thought as what I should come up to the manor with Jack here. I'm afraid I gave the lad too much brandy—to kill the pain it was. And him—not being used to so much, I guess—I suppose that's what's set him off to talking so. For anybody who's rode the London mail will tell you he's a sober lad, for all that he's acting queerer than a sheep with maggots in its head." He continued in a doubtful tone, "I only thought I should make sure you still want him up at the manor."

Cecily looked down at Jack. He had been carried in on a plank and was now half lying, half resting upon one arm. His pallor was worse than she had expected from hearing his words, and she realized what an effort it had cost him to sound so cheery. Her heart went out to him for his bravery and her face flooded with warmth.

"Of course you must leave him," she said to the innkeeper. "My grandfather would not hear of turning him out. And I am certain he will remember his manners once the effects of your excellent brandy have worn off." Mr. Rose looked relieved and bowed his gratitude.

Doctor Whiting claimed her attention. "I am afraid it was a very bad break, Miss Wolverton. I thought it best for him to be brought up here to set it. Then, he ought to be kept quiet for several days. But, as you can see, he is not the most restful of patients." Cecily nodded.

But at the sound of Cecily's voice, Jack had lifted his head, and was now focussing his eyes upon her in a curious manner. Suddenly, there was a glimmer in them, as if he had just then recognized her.

He spoke, directing at Cecily a look which froze her with embarrassment. "'But, soft! what light from yonder window breaks? It is the east, and Juliet is the sun!'"

There was a moment of stunned silence in the room before Mrs. Selby, who already resented the disturbance in her domain, stepped forward and said, "Now, just you mind your manners, young man. That's Miss Cecily you're speaking to and nobody named Juliet. So just you keep your tongue in your head and don't carry on about your betters." She clearly believed Jack had mistaken her mistress for one of his lightskirts and was grossly offended.

But Doctor Whiting was not under the same misapprehension. He raised his eyebrows and regarded Cecily with an enquiring air. "Not the normal conversation of a mail coachman I would say, Miss Wolverton. Would you not agree?"

Cecily was still too stunned by Jack's words to answer with composure, but she nodded and remarked rather breathlessly, "It is odd, surely."

Jack was now leaning upon one elbow, and he extended the other arm out towards her, saying in a slurred voice,

"She speaks:
O, speak again, bright angel! for thou art/As glorious to this night, being o'er my head,
As is a winged messenger of heaven...."

One of the ostlers snickered and clapped his hand over his mouth before Mr. Rose could reprimand him. Cecily blushed to the roots of her hair, while the other men from the inn stared back and forth between her and Jack.

Mrs. Selby, however, was not so paralyzed. "'This night,' indeed!" she scoffed indignantly. "As if it weren't midday and light enough to prove it! He's drunk! That's what he is. I would have expected better from you, Mr. Rose, than to bring a drunken boy what hasn't got any manners up to the manor house!"

Mr. Rose was almost as confused by Jack's behaviour as Cecily was, but he did not appreciate the tone in which he had been addressed. He drew himself up. "I take leave to remind you, Mrs. Selby, that it was Sir Waldo himself who gave orders for the lad to be brought here. Though I will say, Miss Cecily," he said, turning to her, "that if I'd known he was going to carry on this way, I would never have brought him."

Cecily was, by now, quite anxious to be rid of all the men who were gaping at her in confusion. "That is quite all right, Mr. Rose," she said. "It is not your fault. I suppose the—" here she hesitated "—the young man is not himself."

And, as if in proof of this, Jack lay slowly back down upon his plank, muttering to himself, "'I am too bold; 'tis not to me she speaks.'"

This was much more to the innkeeper's liking and he threw Jack a grateful look. "There now. That's right, miss. Jack's a good lad. The guard on the mail thinks the world of him, and that Davies is a hard man to please. Will you be wanting me for anything else?"

"No, nothing, thank you," said Cecily hastily. "If you could just have your men carry him up the stairs to a room—Mrs. Selby will guide you—that will be all." She watched from a safe corner while the ostlers bore Jack up the stairs, but not before he spouted forth another revealing bit of verse.

"'It is my lady; O, it is my love! O, that she knew she were!'"

Now that they were out of sight of the mistress, more of the ostlers gave in to guffaws, and Cecily could hear them echoing down the stairs. She put both hands to her cheeks to cool them, forgetting that Doctor Whiting was standing nearby.

When he spoke, she jumped. "That was a perfect rendering of parts of *Romeo and Juliet*, if I'm not mistaken, Miss Wolverton."

Lowering her hands rapidly, she turned to face him. "I do think you are right, Doctor Whiting." They regarded each other for a moment before she spoke again, and then rather defensively.

"If you think I have any explanation for it, Doctor, you are mistaken."

Doctor Whiting was instantly apologetic. "Of course not, Miss Wolverton. I am sorry if I gave you any reason to think I needed any. It is simply quite peculiar. I suppose the lad might have had an unusual upbringing—perhaps his people were in the theatre. It was just that he seemed to recognize you. I meant no offence by the comment," he added.

Cecily smiled and confessed, "It is quite all right, Doctor. You see, I have seen the young man before. He took me up on the mail and brought me here more than a month ago—though why he should speak to me in such a fashion . . ." She did not finish the sentence. "But I daresay you are correct," she said, "his family must have been in the theatre." She tried to look relieved, but was actually feeling disappointed. For a brief moment, she had allowed herself to think something else.

Doctor Whiting looked at her seriously. "If you had rather not take him into the house, I could find room for him in my lodgings," he suggested. "He would not get the care he would here, but Sir Waldo might not like the thought of an actor, former or otherwise, being loosed in his home."

"Oh, no!" cried Cecily, adding quickly, "My grandfather is quite looking forward to talking to the coachman...about coaching, you understand. Oh, no. I would not like to disappoint him. You must not worry."

Doctor Whiting nodded as if he understood. "All right, then. I'll go up to him now, miss, if that suits you."

Cecily urged him to do just that, adding that he might ask Mrs. Selby for anything he needed. Then she waited until the housekeeper was back downstairs, and gave her orders concerning the young man's belongings.

While these were being carried out, Cecily sought refuge in the parlour to clear her addled thoughts. A coachman who quoted Shakespeare! What manner of man was he? The first time she had seen him, she had been struck by the gentleness of his speech. And now this! Could he be a gentleman? Would a gentleman have any reason to drive a mail coach?

Cecily shook herself roughly, commanding herself to make no more of this foolishness. The doctor had given the most probable answer. Her coachman was nothing more than the son of an actor—or worse, an actor himself. He could hardly be a gentleman, for gentlemen, she knew, regarded coaching as nothing more than a pastime, a lark for those idle enough and rich enough to engage in it. But this man made his living on the box.

Had he really recognized her in his stupor? She devoutly hoped not, for if he were an actor it would be most uncomfortable should he make it his habit to spout forth in such a manner again before the servants. She wondered worriedly whether she had done anything to encourage his behaviour and recalled their brief encounter on the road to her mind. There was the one compliment he had made her, most improperly. But he had not required much in the way of reproof to discourage him, and after that, had been careful not to transgress again. Cecily freely admitted that she was used to being obeyed and approached with respect and had no notion of being treated otherwise. But that did not mean, she told herself, that she would not recognize arrogance and impertinence when she encountered it. The coachman, she believed firmly, had been neither of these. Nor, she concluded, had she done anything untoward to encourage unseemly behaviour.

It was simply that on several occasions he had not seemed to be conscious of the difference between them. Perhaps his parents had raised him with revolutionary principles, as actors were said to do. That could account for it.

But shortly she received another shock, this time at the hands of Mrs. Selby. After completing her duties, the housekeeper found Cecily alone in the parlour and confronted her with two objects, one in each hand.

"I thought you should know, Miss Cecily, that I found these in the young scoundrel's bag when I was unpacking it like you asked me. I set one of the maids to do the unpacking, for I've got better things to do than to occupy myself with a scapegrace's belongings. But Sarah come back down to me and told me she'd found these amongst his things, so I thought I'd better have a look myself. Do you think they've been stolen?"

Cecily took the two small volumes the housekeeper held in her hands. They were covered in the finest brown leather, and she could see that they had been handled with care. Opening them, she found that they were impossible for her to read—for one was in Latin, the other in Greek. Her heart beat strangely.

"No, I do not think they are stolen, Mrs. Selby," she said finally, running her hands softly over the fine bindings. She had seen the inscription inside a front leaf, "To my dear son, Jack," with a signature in a flowing hand. She tried to make out the name, but the signature was too stylized. It was of no consequence.

"Please put these back with his belongings, Mrs. Selby," Cecily said, "and do not say anything more about them. They belong to the coachman." As the older woman made her way back up the stairs, Cecily followed her to Jack's room.

She had given orders for him to be placed in one of the servants' rooms that was not being used at present. There she saw that the doctor was nearly finished with his work. Doctor Whiting was covered with perspiration from trying to set Jack's leg. Jack, she could see as she stepped to the bed, was, unfortunately, still awake. He lay with the back of one hand touching his forehead, his mouth set in a grim line.

"How is he, Doctor?" asked Cecily quietly. Jack's eyes opened and he frowned, as if he was straining to hear her voice.

"It's almost set, Miss Wolverton," answered the doctor with a sigh. "But it's been a fierce one. The poor lad's stuck with me all the way. One more pull now and I ought to have it."

She motioned him to go on and not to let her presence delay him. She was standing near the head of Jack's bed and he was staring at her as if she were a vision. To her consternation, he extended his hand.

She did not take it, but looked round quickly to see whether the doctor had noticed. Doctor Whiting was busy, preparing himself to take the last wrench at Jack's leg. Her eyes returned to Jack, whose hand had fallen back to his forehead. She heard him mumble, "'O, wilt thou leave me so unsatisfied?'"

Suddenly, Doctor Whiting took Jack by the ankle and pulled his leg down sharply. A hiss escaped Jack's lips and his eyes shut in pain. Quickly, without knowing what she did, Cecily grabbed for one of his hands and held it tightly. A moment more, and Jack was unconscious.

The doctor was soon finished and Cecily accompanied him to the landing. He gave her instructions for Mrs. Selby to carry out with respect to Jack's care, and was about to take his leave when Cecily remembered something. "Doctor Whiting," she said after a moment's hesitation, "it might be best if you did not mention to my grandfather what you heard today. There is no need to bother him with speculation, and I am certain from all that is said of the coachman that he won't repeat his earlier behaviour."

Doctor Whiting nodded. "That's all right, then. I won't mention a word to Sir Waldo. You will likely get to the bottom of it. And I doubt," he said with a twinkle, "that Mrs. Selby will know to give the poor lad away."

Remembering the housekeeper's misunderstanding of Jack's words, Cecily smiled and waved goodbye to the doctor.

She returned to her room, where she lay down for an uncustomary rest upon the coverlets. Jack's pain had distressed her. But her heart beat queerly for another reason.

There were his words, of course, so convincingly uttered that he might well have been an actor. But that was not all. Cecily knew for a certainty that he was not an actor. For no actor received instruction in both Latin and Greek.

CHAPTER FIVE

JACK SLEPT SOUNDLY for most of the night, but he awoke to strange surroundings. It took him no more than a moment to remember the accident, for the pain in his leg reminded him of it quickly enough. The ache in his head only made the whole seem worse. For the life of him, he could not remember where he was. He only knew from the look of things that he had been placed in a servant's room somewhere, and that the house was too quiet to be an inn. The nearest window was several feet from the bed, too far for him to see anything below, and it was dark besides.

Jack soon gave up his efforts. He lay awake mostly, dozing occasionally, until a servant girl brought him his breakfast in the morning. She was in a hurry to do her other work and would not stay to answer many of his questions. She did tell him, however, that he had been brought to the home of Sir Waldo Staveley, who would shelter him during his recovery. Jack accepted this gratefully, acknowledging to himself that it was far better than to be left in his lonely lodgings, or even at the inn. His meagre earnings would rapidly be consumed under such circumstances, and he did not intend to notify his father of the incident.

His jaw tensed at the thought, which did nothing to improve his headache. Lying back against the pillows, which the maid had fluffed for him, he closed his eyes and sighed. Oh, to be in the hands of his own valet! Obviously, he had undervalued that poor devil's skills.

After sitting up as well as he could, Jack managed to spoon the best of his porridge down his throat without spilling it. He only wished there were more. He remembered now that the accident had happened in the morning, and he had had nothing to eat since breakfast the day before. The throbbing in his head was testimony to the fact that he had been given much to drink, however, and he would have been grateful for a full stomach to mitigate the effects of the brandy.

He tried to remember something more about the afternoon. What was it? *Oh, yes.* The accident had occurred outside the village where he had dropped off the mysterious lady a month ago. Since that time he had watched out for her each time the mail passed through, but he had never caught a glimpse of her. He had dreamt she was with him last night.

Such foolishness produced a twisted smile, but there was little mirth in it.

There came a knock at the door. He called, "Come in," and waited while it opened. Much to his amazement, the object of his thoughts came walking into the room.

"Good morning," said the vision brightly. She was carrying a tray with a glass of water and some powders. Jack stared at her speechlessly as she went to a table and busied herself with some preparation.

Finally, his silence caused her to raise her eyes to his. Then she lowered them in confusion.

"I am Miss Cecily Wolverton," she explained. "You were injured yesterday and brought up to my grandfather's house. He is Sir Waldo Staveley. Do you remember?"

Jack ignored her statement. "It *was* you!" he said.

She raised her eyes again to him questioningly. "I beg your pardon?" she said.

It was Jack's turn to blush. "Forgive me, Miss... Wolverton," he said, remembering what she had told him. "I am afraid I do not recall much of what happened, but I do recollect seeing you." Then he added softly, "I thought it was a dream."

She turned away from him suddenly and busied herself again with the powder and water. After a few moments of stirring, she brought it to him and told him to drink it. "The doctor left this. It will help to lessen the pain."

But Jack did not wish to take it right away. He held the glass until she released it, promising to drink it soon if she would answer a few of his questions. The name Wolverton sounded vaguely familiar, but he needed his mind clear to be able to place it. She eyed him warily, but did not seem to take offense at his manner.

"You say this is the home of your grandfather?" he asked. "Why have I been brought here?"

Cecily smiled and explained, "My grandfather, Sir Waldo, is a subscriber to the Foundation for the Relief of Indigent Coachmen and their Dependents. He often extends his hospitality to coachmen, and when he heard of your injury, insisted you be brought here to recuperate." Her eyes twinkled. "He likes to have visits from other drivers, and he would be very glad, when you are able, to converse with you about the finer points of driving."

Jack remembered her mentioning something of her grandfather's interest in coaching when she rode on the mail. "Of course," he said. "He must be the grandfather who supplied you with that very useful piece of harness."

Cecily inclined her head. She seemed slightly disturbed by the recollection.

"And do you live here?" Jack asked.

"Yes."

"Then I most certainly shall be happy to converse with him," said Jack, forgetting to remember his station. "Will you be so kind as to give my compliments to Sir Waldo, and thank him for his generosity?"

"And whose name shall I give?" she asked.

This reminded Jack of his situation, and he responded more humbly, "That would be Henley, miss. Jack Henley." He wondered if she had noticed the slip in his manner. It seemed so difficult to remember his circumstances when she was near.

She smiled enigmatically, and Jack suspected that she was more than a little amused.

"I shall be happy to convey your compliments, Mr. Henley. Now I shall leave you to your rest, but if you have any requirements for your comfort, I beg you will tell the girl who is serving you. The doctor wishes you to rest as much as possible."

Jack opened his mouth to protest her leaving, and then closed it again with a frown. She could not be expected to linger at the whim of a coachman, and he had no intention of divulging his true identity.

He lay back in the bed and stared up at the ceiling. This was a strange kettle of fish! To awaken in *her* home, of all places! He could scarcely believe his good fortune. And now he knew her name. *Cecily.* Cecily Wolverton. Miss Wolverton to him now, that was true. But Jack was an optimistic fellow, and he did not worry overmuch about details. He would soon come about, and right now he could rest, content in the knowledge that he was under the same roof as a very intriguing lady. He only wondered why her name should sound familiar to him.

His leg hurt dreadfully, however, so he kept to his promise, drank his laudanum, and drifted off into a happy sleep.

IN THE AFTERNOON he awoke to find his leg throbbing worse than ever. There was no one in the room, but he saw that another tray had been left for him. It carried a bowl of thin soup, nothing more, and it must have been there for some time for the fat had begun to congeal on the liquid's surface. Jack looked at it disgustedly and swore. The pain in his leg was enough to try the best of tempers, and while a substantial meal might have helped his spirits, at least, the soup was an affront to his sensibilities.

There was no way for him to ring for a servant, the servants' rooms not being equipped with bell pulls. But there was a light chair set close to his bed. He reached for it, swearing again as the movement hurt his leg, and began to thump it against the floor.

The sound echoed down through the manor, and before long he heard quick steps coming up the stairs, followed by some heavier ones.

"Lord on us, Mr. Henley!" cried the girl who had brought him his porridge that morning upon entering the room. "Whatever is the matter? You'll have the whole house down on us!"

Jack frowned at the poor girl. He had allowed himself to hope that the steps he had heard belonged to her mistress.

"My leg hurts. That's what the matter is," he said. "And I am hungry. Would you please fetch your mistress and tell her I would be grateful for some more laudanum?"

An offended voice came from the doorway, "That will not be necessary, young man." Mrs. Selby had followed the maid up the stairs and was puffing in indignation at the door. "Miss Cecily gave me instructions you was to have another dose when you woke. There'll be no need to disturb her. You can have it and go back to sleep after you've had your broth."

She approached his bed with a glass.

Now this was not what Jack wanted. "I thank you, whoever you are," he said irritably, "But I must insist that you call your mistress. I want a word with her."

Mrs. Selby turned red in the face. "I am Mrs. Selby, if you please. Housekeeper to Sir Waldo Staveley. And I'll have none of your cheek." She began to grumble, "Coming in here and raising such a rumpus. You ought to be ashamed!"

Jack bit back a retort. He reminded himself that these people knew nothing of him other than that he was a mail coach driver.

"I beg your pardon, Mrs. Selby," he said more cordially. "But I would be extremely grateful if you would ask your mistress if I might have a word with her."

The housekeeper looked at him suspiciously. "And why would you be needing to talk to Miss Cecily? Not to repeat them things you said to her yesterday, I hope?"

Jack was startled. "Yesterday? What did I say yesterday?"

Mrs. Selby would not oblige him. She looked as if she would like to, but for some reason could not repeat his words. "Never you mind," was all she said. "But you were that disrespectful."

"I was?" asked Jack, thoroughly mystified. He had never spoken disrespectfully to a lady in his life. And if he had, why had Miss Cecily given no sign of being offended? He decided Mrs. Selby was exaggerating and dismissed it.

"Well, never mind that now. I, of course, shall be most respectful to your mistress. But would you please send someone to fetch her. I really am in the most intolerable pain."

Now Mrs. Selby was not a hard woman, but neither did she think Miss Cecily should be waiting on a common coachman. She tried to get Jack to drink his laudanum, but he refused. Then she tried to coax him with his soup, but he complained it was too cold. In frustration, she told him that if it were left to her she would let him lie and rot, but Miss Cecily had left her orders that he was to be made comfortable.

"Then ask her to come here, please, and I will be a good boy," said Jack wearily.

Mrs. Selby noticed the firm set of his mouth. There was something about him she mistrusted, but she had lived long enough to respect determination wherever she saw it. She also knew that Jack's chalky pallor was caused by extreme pain.

Without a word then, she nodded to the servant girl, who ran out of the room. Then she rose ponderously from her chair and started towards the door, looking back only to deliver these final words: "All right, young man. But just so you'll know, I'll be right outside here in the corridor if Miss Cecily needs me."

Jack closed his eyes and sighed in relief, but he did wonder what he had said yesterday to make Mrs. Selby so wary of him. Perhaps the pain had made him curse. He must apologize to Cecily if he had said anything rude.

After a few minutes, Cecily entered. She must have come quickly to arrive so soon, he reflected, and now that she was there he felt sheepish. She eyed him with concern as she stood by the bed.

"What is the matter, Mr. Henley? Sarah said you would not take your medicine."

She looked young and fresh standing there, in a green muslin gown which hugged her neat figure. Feeling curiously better, Jack stared for a moment before answering.

"I am sorry, Miss Cecily, for disturbing you, but I must ask a favour of you."

"Yes, what is it?" she said. She did not seem to be offended.

"Might I have..." he began. It sounded so silly, really. "Might I have something to eat?"

Her eyes widened in shock. "Haven't you had anything, Mr. Henley? Oh, I am so very sorry! But I brought you in a bowl of soup myself!"

"You did?" asked Jack, peculiarly pleased. "Well, yes, the soup was here when I awoke. But, you see, it was very cold by that time and I could not eat it."

"Naturally," she said, quite contrite. "I should have left instructions for it to be heated and brought to you later. You were so sound asleep, you see, when I brought it, that I did not like to have you disturbed. I thought you would wake soon. Would you like to have it brought now?"

Jack directed her a pleading look. "No, not exactly. I was wondering whether I might not have something more substantial. You see, my leg may be injured, but I assure you, my stomach is perfectly unharmed."

Cecily looked blankly at him for one moment and then laughed. "Oh, I see. I am so sorry, Mr. Henley. You must be starving! Well, I had quite thought you would be feeling too poorly to eat. I shall have something brought up to you quickly. But you must take your laudanum. Mrs. Selby told me you were in pain."

Jack shifted uncomfortably and saw her wince in sympathy.

"I can't very well do that or I shall fall asleep before my food gets here," he said.

She frowned, thinking for a moment. Then she said, "You must take it. It will take a short while to take effect, and I will engage to stay with you to keep you awake until you have eaten."

Jack readily agreed to this arrangement, so Cecily stepped out into the hall to order his meal. Then he behaved docilely as she handed him his medicine.

The dosage was not really so strong as to put him to sleep, but he did not bother to tell his companion. She sat down upon the small chair, which seemed perfectly suited to hold her, and folded her hands. Remembering what Mrs. Selby had reported, Jack cleared his throat and ventured, "Miss Cecily, when I was brought in, I hope I did not say anything particularly offensive. If I did, I hope you will pardon me on the grounds that I was not myself."

Her brows lifted. "Offensive? I do not recall that you said anything offensive, Mr. Henley."

Jack sighed inwardly with relief. "That's all right, then. Mrs. Selby said . . . But never mind. It must not have been anything."

At this comment, Cecily smiled rather secretively and he was left to wonder at the source of her amusement.

"You must tell me about your work, Mr. Henley," she suggested. So Jack told her about being a driver on the London to Birmingham mail, and as he talked, the laudanum began to take effect, his leg hurt less, and he forgot for a while who he was pretending to be. If Cecily noticed anything unusual in the manner in which he discussed his employment, however, she kept it to herself.

A servant brought in a heavily laden tray and set it beside him. Cecily watched as Jack was given a large plate of roast mutton, boiled potatoes and turnips, with pudding and ale. It was a meal for a hungry labourer, but Jack did not mind that, for he had just such an appetite.

Much to his satisfaction, Cecily stayed while he ate and sat until the last bite crossed his lips. Then she rose and removed the tray to one side.

"There now, Mr. Henley," she said. "I trust you will be able to sleep. From now on, I shall give orders that you are to be fed regularly at mealtimes. And if there is anything amiss, you must just say so."

Jack did not like the note of finality in her voice, so he said, "But how am I to call anyone? I do not like to be thumping the floor for the servants whenever I am in need of something."

Cecily's lips twitched. "No, you must not do that. I shall see that you are given a bell."

"Perhaps it would be better if you brought me my laudanum yourself, Miss Cecily," Jack suggested, doing his best to maintain a look of innocence. "That is, I would not trust the servants with it if I were you."

"Ah," said Cecily with the hint of a smile about her lips. "I admit that had not occurred to me. I shall have to think it over. Mrs. Selby could be trusted to bring it, however."

Jack tried to sit up in protest, and then cursed his impulsiveness as his leg moved.

"Mr. Henley!" cried Cecily, hurrying back to him. "You must be more careful!"

Jack spoke through gritted teeth, "It is just that I should not like to inconvenience Mrs. Selby. I should not feel right to know I had disrupted Sir Waldo's household."

"Perhaps you are right," agreed Cecily quickly. "I shall bring your laudanum to you myself. Twice a day," she assured him. Jack had not planned this particular ruse, but it had been effective.

When the pain in his leg had subsided again, Cecily moved towards the door. "Oh, Mr. Henley," she said, turning before leaving, "were you ever in an acting troupe, or were your parents actors?"

Jack started in amazement. "Actors? Certainly not. Why?"

She smiled. "I just wondered. From something you said, but . . . never mind." She gave him another secretive smile and then closed the door behind her.

"Actors?" said Jack to himself. His mind was beginning to fog over from the combination of laudanum and ale, and the fullness of his stomach was inducing sleep. Why should she think he was an actor? That was worse than being thought a coachman! He frowned, his eyes closed. What could he have said to make her suspect that? Confound it! What had he said yesterday?

THE QUESTION continued to plague Jack in his dreams. But the following three weeks were a greater trial to him as he spent the main part of his days in unrelieved solitude. He was well fed and made as comfortable as could be, but there was little he could do to combat his boredom. The highlights of his days were the two visits from Cecily, morning and evening, when she would come to bring his medicine. Jack did his best to prolong these visits, thinking up excuses to keep her there as long as possible. And he did not tell her when the pain in his leg stopped requiring the use of laudanum. He just held the glass until she left the room, and then poured the contents into his chamber pot.

Once Cecily suggested that Mrs. Selby might take over the duty of these visits, but Jack protested vehemently that he was quite afraid of Mrs. Selby.

"She has taken me into an unaccountable dislike, Miss Cecily," he said plaintively. "I'm afraid she might try to poison me." Some time since, Jack had conveniently forgotten to use Cecily's surname and had adopted the style of address used by her grandfather's old retainers. She had not bothered to correct him.

"Poison you, Mr. Henley! I assure you she would do nothing of the kind! You cannot be quite rational if you can imagine such a thing."

Jack feigned innocence though his blue eyes danced with merriment. He would have liked to say how much *her* visits meant to him, and how much he looked forward to them. But he had not forgotten the one time he had overstepped his bounds when speaking to her on the mail. Her look of reproach had stayed with him, and he would not like to see it repeated.

"That must be it," he said, putting his hand to his brow. "I must be feverish. But please don't leave me to Mrs. Selby. The fright would not be good for a man in my condition. Who knows what I might not do?"

For a moment he was certain that she had seen through his ruse, but she disguised her mirth with a hasty cough and rose to leave.

"Very well, then, Mr. Henley. I shall continue to bring your medicine myself, although I cannot think you will be requiring it much longer." She ignored Jack's sheepish grin and continued, "But you must be quite bored lately with nothing to do all day but stare at the walls. It is too bad you do not read."

"Read?" said Jack eagerly. He had not liked to ask for books, knowing it would be a most peculiar request, coming from a servant of the road.

At the sound of his tone, however, she gave him an enquiring look. "Do you mean to say you are a reading man, Mr. Henley?"

Jack flushed uncomfortably. "Yes, of course. That is, I know my letters, and I... Yes, I am," he finished lamely.

"Well," said Cecily, evidently much surprised. "Then I shall see about sending you up some books to read. That will be much better than having you fret with boredom. You might get up to mischief, and we mustn't have that leg injured again now, must we?"

Something in her tone made Jack look at her suspiciously, but her manner was simply that of an efficient nurse. He thanked her humbly.

The books were sent up and they were quite a relief to Jack, although he was still unused to such inactivity. In some ways he would have preferred to be back on the box, driving the mail. But, at the same time, he knew that returning to his job would mean losing Cecily's companionship entirely. And he had discovered that there was much pleasure to be derived from the companionship of a pert young lady.

CHAPTER SIX

REFLECTIONS ABOUT THE LADY of the house had begun to occupy his thoughts excessively, when one day he was surprised by a visit. It was midmorning, not Cecily's customary time to look in upon him. She knocked and then entered, accompanied by an elderly manservant carrying a crutch.

"Good morning again, Mr. Henley," she greeted him. "I have come to request a favour of you. My grandfather has been waiting to have a chat with you and I thought, if you were feeling up to it, you might like to come along to his room right now."

Jack sat up quickly and said, "I should be delighted, Miss Cecily, er, Miss Wolverton," he corrected, seeing the frown on the servant's face. "I cannot promise to make it on my own, but I shall do my best."

"I've brought Selby to help you," said Cecily. "You must not hurt yourself. You can lean on his arm and use the crutch to lift your leg. I have already spoken to the doctor and he said you might try getting up and about if you're careful."

Jack eagerly reached for the crutch and rose, putting his weight on his good foot, only to waver slightly as dizziness threatened to overcome him. He laughed with embarrassment. "I am as weak as a newborn, Miss Wolverton. I hope I shall not disgrace myself in front of your grandfather."

He was even more concerned about falling on his face in front of her, but she put out a hand to steady him and it buoyed him considerably. "Please do not undertake it if you are not able," she pleaded. He liked the sound of concern in her voice.

"It's nothing now," he said smiling. "Just a little shaky at first, that's all. Shall we go?"

They made their way slowly down the corridor. Fortunately, Sir Waldo's house was built so that the servants had their own wing, and the principal bedrooms were on the same floor as Jack's. They had only to negotiate the length of the servants' wing and the turn between it and the main corridor before they approached Sir Waldo's quarters.

Jack found his strength returning, and with each step he took he learned how to manage the crutch better. Before long he was not relying much upon Selby's arm and could remark laughingly, "Well, Selby, I am much obliged for your assistance, but the next time why don't we see if I can't hop the whole way."

He did not win the servant's respect by saying this; however, for the old man replied, "That's *Mr.* Selby to you, you young upstart. You'll not be using your disrespect with me!"

Jack, thus put properly in his place, humbly begged Selby's pardon, and with an abashed glance at Cecily, prepared to meet her grandfather.

Sir Waldo was sitting up in his bed and, as Jack entered, he regarded him fixedly through his quizzing glass. Jack felt quite suddenly as though he were undergoing inspection by the Postmaster General himself, and hastily decided he had better mind his manners if he wanted to be invited again. He straightened self-consciously and left his impudence at the door.

"Here is Mr. Henley to see you, Grandpapa," said Cecily.

"Jack, sir," he amended.

"Please sit down, Jack," said Sir Waldo. "And relieve that leg of yours. Glad to see you're up on your feet. Though not quite able to handle a team of four yet, I'll warrant."

Jack smiled and began to lower himself into a chair, but was stopped by the intrusion of the soft muzzle of a dog between himself and his intended seat. Sir Waldo's ancient hunting bitch had come to inspect the visitor.

"Here, Leto! Come away from there! Let the poor boy sit," called Sir Waldo.

The dog abandoned her activity with reluctance, but stiffly moved to obey her master. Jack was intrigued by her name.

"Leto, sir?" he asked with raised brows, forgetting he would not be expected to recognize the mother of Apollo and Artemis.

Fortunately, Sir Waldo did not detect the amusement in his voice and answered with an explanation. "A Greek goddess, my boy. Something you wouldn't know. I named her that because she was always wandering about looking for a place to pup."

Jack hid his appreciation of Sir Waldo's wit and arranged his face into a suitable expression of mild bewilderment. His host ignored it and turned the conversation to a subject he thought more appropriate. While Jack listened, Sir Waldo told him about his own driving days as an amateur in the Benson Driving Club, relaying such stories as he thought would appeal to a younger coachman. As they talked, Jack remembered to thank Sir Waldo for the contraption that had saved him from incurring a fine the day Cecily had ridden with him on the box. Sir Waldo tut-tutted, but not without an air of pride.

Jack found Sir Waldo to be pleasant company, and was grateful for this respite from his solitude. Cecily, he was glad to see, had taken a chair by her grandfather's bed and was doing some handwork while they chatted. She looked upon them with tolerant amusement, but he fancied that she regarded him from time to time with a certain curiosity.

After a good hour spent discussing the merits of various harnesses and their makers, all kinds of tack, and the fascinating quirks of coach horses and solutions to their behaviour, Sir Waldo lay back with a satisfied sigh. He looked Jack over approvingly.

"Did you say your father was a coachman before you, my boy?"

Jack smothered a grin and replied, "Not exactly, sir. But he was very much occupied with horses in one way or another."

Sir Waldo nodded confidently. "I knew you were bred to it. A fellow coachman can always tell." He missed the twinkle in Jack's eye and continued his questions. "How long have you been at it then?"

"Just four months."

"Four months!" The old man raised his eyebrows. "Well, I daresay you were an ostler for quite a long while before moving up. But you must have had some fine fellows to emulate, eh?"

Jack thought of old Jem, his father's coachman, who had let him take the reins whenever Jack wanted to cut a lark. "Yes, sir," he said. "I did."

Sir Waldo was looking tired, but he was not ready to let Jack go. "Well, you are a fine lad," he said. "It is a great measure of comfort to me, in the condition in which I now find myself, to realize that my time as an amateur coachman was not wasted."

"Sir?" Jack was puzzled.

Sir Waldo went on as if he had not spoken. "To know that by our small efforts—my friends, and mine, mind you—a kind word here and there, a bit of guidance, some discussion on the nobler aspects of your craft—lads like you can be influenced to turn out as well-spoken and sensible as you have. You would not countenance now, I suppose, the sort of language one met with when taking the mail back when it was started. But now, I understand that a lady may take the mail—or even the stage, if she were so desperate—without running the risk of being insulted or offended."

Jack listened in amazed silence.

"My granddaughter spoke of you after you brought her here," continued Sir Waldo. "And while that was an extraordinary escapade, for which I spoke quite firmly to her..." He tossed a reproving look in Cecily's direction. "She spoke quite highly of your manners and your bearing. The Royal Mail should be proud."

These words made Jack blush more rosily than he had ever done in his life. He had already been mentally writhing under the falsehood of his position, and could not bear the praise being heaped upon him. It would be one thing, he thought, if he had merited Sir Waldo's words, but quite another for the son of a baronet to be accepting praise for speaking well!

He ventured a look at Cecily, who had suddenly jumped up from her chair and, with her back turned towards him, was smoothing Sir Waldo's covers. He could only be glad she had not noticed his discomfort.

Fortunately, at this point, Sir Waldo indicated that he was ready for Jack to retire. The conversation had been entertaining, but had provided more excitement than he was now accustomed to. Selby advanced to assist his master to recline, and Jack stood up alone, waving away the suggestion of any help back to his room.

After bidding Sir Waldo goodbye, he hobbled through the door held by Cecily. Until he stood, he had not realized how tired he was himself, and the support of Selby's arm would have been very useful at that moment. But Jack could not very well ask for it, having assured the room at large that he did not require it. Using only one crutch gave him a tendency to swivel more than he would like, and his progress back to his room was slow.

Cecily walked alongside him in order to open the doors to the corridors. She watched his progress anxiously.

"A fine old gentleman, your grandfather," said Jack once they had got out of his hearing. "He knows quite a bit about horses."

Cecily smiled at him gratefully. "Thank you so much for going to him. You cannot know how much it means to Grandpapa to keep in touch with the drivers on the road. Not a day goes by that he does not mention when the coach should be arriving." Her eyes lit mischievously. "He always sends a footman down for any letters, but I really think it is to see if the mail has come on time!"

Jack chuckled. "Your grandfather is not the only curious one. He puts me in mind of the young boys I take up occasionally. Always wanting to know my best times, and if I race carriages when I am not driving the mail. They are most disappointed to learn that when I have finished my run, all I want then, of course, is a good, full meal and a nice bed! Oh, well," he added, "I was much the same, I suppose."

Cecily regarded him curiously. "Were you?" she asked.

Jack answered unguardedly, "My heavens, yes! Up to any kind of foolishness, I was. That was before—" He broke off suddenly and turned his head to see her reaction, but the quick movement of his head threw him off balance, and he started to fall upon his bad leg.

Cecily moved swiftly to his side and threw an arm about his waist, just as his broken leg touched the floor. Jack gasped and then swore, closing his eyes tightly for an interval until the pain abated. When he opened them, it was to find Cecily, still with one arm around him, peeking up at him anxiously from under his arm.

Jack smiled at her apologetically. "I'm so sorry, Cecily. You must excuse my manners, but that hurt like the very devil." She blushed, and he realized he had forgotten to address her properly. Still, she did not remove her support.

"That's perfectly all right," she assured him, struggling to keep her composure in this awkward position. "I daresay I should be swearing if my leg were in a similar case."

"And I should be very surprised," said Jack by way of a compliment, but at Cecily's sudden frown, he realized he had once again overstepped his bounds and dropped the subject at once.

She had withdrawn her arm from his back, but was still standing near to him. Now she asked, "Will you be quite all right, or shall I give you my arm?"

Jack supposed he ought to have tried to make it on his own, but the truth was his leg still hurt dreadfully. And he found he liked the feel of Cecily's touch.

He winced purposefully and her arm went quickly round him again. "If I could just put one hand on your shoulder..." he suggested. She did not refuse, so he wrapped his whole arm around her and leaned slightly against her. She would not look up.

They started down the corridor again, and Jack tried not to put too much of a burden on her slender frame. The top of her head came just to his chin, and her soft curls tickled him occasionally as they brushed against it.

They scarcely spoke, for both were intent upon acting as if nothing were out of the ordinary. He wished he could remove some of her embarrassment by telling her who he really was, but knew that he must not. After all, he thought grimly, he was not Sir Geoffrey Henley's son until his father chose to recognize him as such.

They were about to reach the door to his room, when Jack addressed her suddenly, "Miss Wolverton, if you don't mind my asking, why *did* you take the mail coach that morning?"

Cecily looked up at him quickly and then released him. He could tell the memory of that occasion still discomposed her. "Why..." she began, as if at a loss. "It was simply that I had to leave my aunt's house very suddenly, and I could not wait for my grandfather's coach to arrive."

"I see," said Jack when she appeared to have stopped. He waited for her to elaborate, but she did not. And he could not insist upon it if she did not wish to tell him. Yet, he felt convinced that something unpleasant must have caused her to flee her aunt's house.

He wished, though, that she would tell him what the matter had been and silently cursed his unlucky position for it prevented any confidences between them.

Cecily raised her chin and looked at him squarely, "So you see, Mr. Henley, that I have been greatly indebted to you for that service." She lowered her eyes again and Jack understood. She would have him think it was in return for that service that she had been so kind to him today.

He was obliged to accept her reason. "T'was nothing, Miss Cecily," he said, reverting to the address of a faithful servant. "And I have been more than amply repaid." He bowed to her with difficulty and then hobbled to his bed. She closed the door softly behind him.

Jack lay down, releasing a great sigh of weariness, and stared up at the ceiling. He thought about the experience he had just had, and feelings of pride, shame, elation, and longing swept through him. Then he thought of Sir Waldo's final words to him about how well he proved the beneficial influence of gentlemen on the road.

All of a sudden, the humour of his situation outweighed all the rest, and Jack opened his mouth and laughed. Soon his whole body shook with the relief of laughter.

Cecily, who had remained outside in the corridor, lost in a reverie, was startled by the sound. At first, distressed and not quite believing what she heard, she put her ear to the door and listened. Yes, it was laughter. She coloured and wondered what Jack could have found to laugh about. She devoutly hoped it was nothing to do with her. She listened again and the laughter subsided. Surely if it were she he was laughing at, he could not sound so heartily amused! No. If Jack were the sort of fellow she now thought him, there would be no harm in his humour.

She found herself smiling as well and wishing she could be inside enjoying the joke with him. She had had little to laugh about in the past two years. But she did not begrudge Jack his pleasure, for she hoped that someday she would know what it was all about. She only wondered why he was pretending not to be a gentleman. By now, she was certain of his being one. He had given himself away too many times during their visits for there to be any doubt about it. His manners, his speech, the frequency with which he forgot to appear humble, all these things proclaimed him as such. She was not taken in by his innocent looks and his devices for keeping her in his room. Only someone who was her social equal would have had the audacity to do the things he had done. A little smile played about her lips as she thought of his artifice. Was it his tricks that had him so amused?

None too soon, she remembered that she ought to be wary of anyone posing as something he was not. And she cautioned herself not to be taken in by his charm. Who could know why he had become a coachman? Had he sunk beneath disgrace? Was he dishonourable?

Her heart answered no. She was certain that was not the case. Surely a dishonourable person in his circumstances would have taken the twenty shillings she had offered him on the mail. That was all the proof she needed. And, despite her certainty that he was gently born, he had never once tried to insinuate himself into the household in any way. He had made no claims he could not substantiate. In a way this confounded her all the more. It suggested that his current occupation was the one in which he expected to stay. The idea was somehow disturbing.

That he enjoyed her company, that he did his utmost to prolong her visits, she was well aware. But that might be only because he was so alone. The thought that he sought her company only to relieve his loneliness somehow left her feeling quite dismal. Yet the memory of his antics to prevent her from leaving his room exhilarated her to an equal degree. Her own rather cheerless circumstances and lack of companionship must clearly be to blame, she thought. She must guard herself from becoming too intrigued by this mysterious coachman.

FOR THE NEXT TWO WEEKS, Jack was called upon daily to make the walk to Sir Waldo's rooms. Each of those times, Cecily came to accompany him, but she was always careful to have a footman with her, both coming and going. Jack thought he understood. To give her assistance, as she had when there was no possibility of another, was excusable. To allow it to happen again would not be. Her manner to him had always been most proper, and if, at times, she accorded him more respect than might have been expected, he had to suppose it was to indulge an invalid. At times he wished she were not so careful. He noticed she was invariably polite and considerate to all the servants, and he could detect little difference between her treatment of them and her kindness to himself. The thought was lowering.

One day, however, as he waited to be fetched, Mr. Selby entered the room. Cecily was not with him.

"You are to come to the master's room at once," he said to Jack without preamble.

Jack stood up quickly, his expression changing rapidly from expectation to concern. "Is anything the matter with Miss Cecily? Sir Waldo?"

But a haughty Mr. Selby would not answer him. He sniffed and commanded Jack to come at once if he knew what was good for him. Jack obliged him, leaving his questioning for those more inclined to answer, for he reasoned that if anything were terribly wrong with either his master or mistress, Selby would not look so smug.

The trip down the corridor was not so arduous now, and within minutes Jack was knocking upon Sir Waldo's door.

"Come in!" roared Sir Waldo in a voice Jack had not heard before.

Sir Waldo was sitting up in bed in a fuming attitude, with Cecily at his side. It looked as if she had been trying to calm him. Jack gave a quick sigh of relief when he saw they were both well. Beyond this he had no time to think.

"Young man!" began Sir Waldo in a stern voice. "I demand an explanation!" He glared accusingly at Jack from beneath his furrowed brow.

"Sir?" asked Jack, at a loss. He glanced quickly at Cecily for enlightenment, but found none. She was regarding him composedly without a hint of emotion to guide him.

Sir Waldo responded angrily, "Do not play the fool with me, if you please. I have here—" he waved a sheet of paper in his hand upon which Jack thought he detected a familiar signature "—I have here a letter from a Sir Geoffrey Henley, Baronet, asking after the welfare of his only son, Jack."

Jack shot another look in Cecily's direction and found that she was barely restraining a smile.

"Yes, sir?" Jack enquired respectfully, facing Sir Waldo once again with confidence.

His response did not please her grandfather, however. "Well, what is it, boy? Are you the son of this gentleman who has written me, or are you a driver on the Royal Mail?"

Jack grinned with just a touch of sheepishness. "Well . . . both, I suppose, sir. That is, if Sir Geoffrey is good enough to claim me."

Sir Waldo's ire mounted. "A bastard, is it! Do you mean to say I have been harbouring this gentleman's bastard in my household! Someone he himself does not recognize. . . ." But Jack's upheld hand and hoot of laughter stopped Sir Waldo before he could finish.

"Please pardon me, Sir Waldo," he said, "for not making myself clearer. But I will overlook the unintended slight to my mother and give you my assurances that I am Sir Geoffrey's legal and natural progeny. All of it, I might add. It is just that my father and I have lately been . . . what one might call estranged."

Sir Waldo's wrath subsided somewhat upon hearing this clarification. "Estranged, are you? On what grounds? If you come into my house in such a disguise, concealing the circumstances of your birth, I feel I have a right to know the truth of the matter."

"Certainly you do, sir," agreed Jack more humbly. "And I meant no disrespect in deceiving you. It was just that I did not feel I should claim what Sir Geoffrey was not pleased to recognize. You see . . ." He looked at Cecily once again. It was one thing to own up to his mistakes to Sir Waldo, and quite another to confess them to his granddaughter. Jack was not proud of what he had to relate.

Cecily, however, was regarding him sympathetically, and with a hint of curiosity, so he took courage and went on, "It was a matter of debts, sir. Excessive debts. My father was of the opinion that some time spent working for a living might give me a greater respect for what I had been born with."

"A wastrel, eh?" asked the old man.

Jack stiffened slightly, but replied with restraint, "If you will, sir."

His manly answer softened Sir Waldo and brought an understanding gleam to his eyes. "Gambling, I suppose," he said more kindly. "Well, boys will be boys. I must say, your father goes about curing profligacy in a rather unique way. A bit of rusticating ought to do the trick just as well—or it did for me," he admitted with a chuckle.

Then, determined not to let Jack off too lightly, he frowned and added, "All the same, young fellow, you had no right to come among us and accept our hospitality without informing us. To think I have allowed my granddaughter to converse with you without heed of the proprieties..."

Jack cut him off again, this time more forcefully. Cecily had uttered a sound of protest. "I beg your pardon, Sir Waldo, but with respect to Miss Wolverton, I have conducted myself as a gentleman would under any circumstances. You can have nothing there with which to reproach me. If I caused you a moment's apprehension, I am truly sorry, but the truth is that I am a driver of the Royal Mail and intend to remain one. If I know my father, he has made no mention in that letter of my returning to his side. He will expect me to carry on, and has merely taken steps to assure himself of my continued existence."

He waited for Sir Waldo's answer, which was reluctantly given. "That is correct, my boy," said the gentleman, visibly abashed. Then, after a pause he added, "But we cannot have Sir Geoffrey's son staying in our servants' quarters now, can we, Cecily?"

Before she could speak, Jack said quickly, "In that case, Sir Waldo, I shall be happy to remove to an inn. But I thank you sincerely for all you have done for me."

Sir Waldo became angry again. "What do you take me for, boy? A pinchfarthing? I only meant you ought to be given one of the guest bedrooms!"

Jack protested that he was more than comfortable where he was, and that he would not allow Sir Waldo to do more than he already had to shelter him. But the old man was adamant. "Nonsense, Jack," he said finally, near again to losing his temper. "You must be moved at once. And you will take your dinner in this room with me. Cecily will act as hostess. Let us have no more of this play-acting. You shall be doing me a favour."

When it was put like that, and since Jack could see that Cecily herself favoured the change, he could not object. He did point out that he had no proper clothes to dine at a gentleman's table, but Sir Waldo did not consider that of material importance. With a wink, he gave Jack to understand that he had done queerer things in his day than to sit down to table in his riding clothes. Jack laughed, and desisted, and straightaway his things were moved to the guest bedroom.

CHAPTER SEVEN

JACK COULD NOT BE SORRY for the change in his accommodation or status. It was true that he had lately been comfortable enough but he could not deny the immediate benefits of being recognized as a gentleman. Mr. and Mrs. Selby, who had been informed of the change and told Jack's deception was due to a delicate family matter, had been forced to change their attitude towards him. Selby might never come to regard him with anything approaching respect, but Mrs. Selby was openly curious. If she had speculations of her own, however, about the young gentleman, she kept them to herself, a rare occurrence indeed.

That first evening, a table for two was set up in Sir Waldo's room alongside his bed where he was taking a tray. When Jack arrived at the time he had been bidden—washed, combed, and shaved at Mr. Selby's hands—Cecily was already seated at the table. Sir Waldo looked quite elegant in a brocade dressing gown. Leto lay curled up before the fire. Sir Waldo regarded Jack expectantly.

"Not too bad an appearance for a coachman, eh, Cecily?" he joked. "I see Selby has made you the loan of one of my neckcloths. You are welcome to them. I have no use for them now and, truth to say, never could abide them. Always interfered with my driving. It's hard to watch the road when your neck's done up like a laced boot."

Jack took a seat opposite Cecily and they exchanged smiling glances. He had never seen her in candlelight, for she had always taken care to come to his room before dusk. Now, in the softly reflected light, she appeared to glow with an inner radiance. The amusement in her eyes only served to make her sparkle the more. Jack felt strangely that, despite his many adventures, he had never experienced a more extraordinary occurrence than sitting down to table with this lady, her in her evening finery, and himself dressed as her servant. In spite of Sir Waldo's protective presence, he could easily imagine they were alone in the room.

But Sir Waldo dominated the conversation, as was his habit. He loved to talk, and when the recipient of his wisdom was as well versed in the things he loved as Jack, there was no restraining him. He kept the conversation centred upon horses: their prices; good qualities in wheelers and leaders; and the fastest times to be achieved between villages. Jack wished he could include Cecily in their talk, but she seemed to be satisfied just to listen, and only occasionally gave him an amused look, as if to say, "Humour him, please. It makes me happy to see him so lively."

Only once during the evening did Cecily venture a comment, and that was when Sir Waldo began asking Jack about his driving escapades while at Oxford.

"Did you act in any Shakespeare when you were at Oxford, Mr. Henley?" she asked.

Her question startled him. "Why, yes, I did," he admitted. "I played Romeo. It was a terrible performance, as I recall," he added, chuckling. "The present Lord Beasley played Juliet."

Cecily put her napkin quickly to her mouth and smothered a laugh. He wondered what she had found to be so funny, for he doubted she was acquainted with Beasley, who now measured over six feet in height and even then had had a heavy beard.

"Pardon me, Mr. Henley," she said when she had recovered. "It is just that something suddenly struck me as funny. But it was not the idea of your performance; I am certain you were quite competent as Romeo." She smiled at him as though she would like to continue laughing at his expense, and Jack returned her smile with a challenge.

"What made you ask if I had read Shakespeare, Miss Wolverton?" he asked.

Cecily strove for an air of innocence, but failed. "Oh, it was nothing. Simply that you recited a few lines the day you were brought into the manor. The ostlers from the inn thought you were too much under the influence of drink, and Mrs. Selby thought... well, she thought something else. Shakespeare, you know," she finished, "has not been part of her education."

"Humph!" said Sir Waldo. "A fine conversation for a coachman on the mail that was. You never said anything about that to me, Cecily."

Cecily lowered her eyes in confusion. "No, I did not, Grandpapa. To tell the truth, I merely thought Mr. Henley had had a most particular upbringing. I did not think you should be bothered with it."

Sir Waldo smiled indulgently. "Naughty puss!"

Then dismissing the topic, he continued to question Jack and to give him advice until the evening was much advanced. After tea had been drunk, he admitted the lateness of the hour and begged to be excused. Jack and Cecily passed together out of the room and strolled slowly down the corridor. Jack could now move soundly on his crutch with no assistance.

"Miss Cecily," began Jack staunchly, for this time he was determined not to be put off. "Something tells me I made a complete ass of myself when those men carried me in here. Can you deny it?"

A laugh escaped her before she answered, "Of course you did not. You were only *very* funny."

Jack bowed, smiling; his vanity was only slightly wounded. "Happy to have amused you, madam."

But Cecily would not allow him to be offended. "No, no, you misunderstand me!" she protested. "Surely I did not find your evident pain amusing, nor your efforts to remain gallant under such—difficult circumstances. It was only your rendering of Shakespeare under the influence of Mr. Rose's medicinal brandy that provided the much needed comedy. But I assure you that you were neither foolish nor anything but very courageous."

Jack's self-respect returned in measure. "Let us hope so," he said, dismissing it. "I will not ask you what lines I delivered that night. I can only be horrified at the thought. But I will ask you what you thought when you heard them, and why you did not tell your grandfather?"

Cecily took a few steps in silence before she confessed reluctantly, "I must admit I thought you a gentleman. Doctor Whiting supposed you might have been an actor. But when the maid unpacked your things and found two books, one in Greek and one in Latin, I could not think otherwise."

"Ah," replied Jack, enlightened. "So all this time, you knew...."

Cecily protested again, "But I could not be certain! Mrs. Selby thought you must have stolen the books." She smiled mischievously.

Jack laughed. "As if anyone would. And I thought I was being so clever...." He sighed with mock disappointment, and Cecily smiled again.

They continued on their walk until the end of the passage signalled the parting of their ways.

"I shall send a footman to wait on you this evening and in the morning," she told him. "Selby must devote most of his time to my grandfather, but he will assist you with your shaving and whatever else you think necessary." She paused, as if uncertain how to go on.

Thinking she must be waiting for his reply, Jack said, "There will be no need. I can very well shave myself. And the footman's services should be enough to help me dress."

He could see that this was not what concerned her. Indeed, he perceived that something was causing her acute embarrassment. "You must not trouble yourself about my comfort," he said, trying to help her. "I shall go on perfectly well."

She smiled at him gratefully. But her next speech was accompanied by a flush of self-consciousness. "I shall ask Mrs. Selby to bring you your laudanum," she told him quickly. "I really ought not to..." She could not find the proper words.

Immediately Jack grasped her difficulty. She ought not to come to his room now that he was known to be an eligible person. "Please don't bother," he said. "I do not really need it any more. In fact," he added, a bold gleam in his eye, "I have not drunk it any time these past three weeks."

Cecily gasped and her eyes flew to his face. There was surprise in them, but no outrage. They were quickly lowered, but a little smile hovered about her lips.

"You ought to be ashamed, Mr. Henley," she said primly. "But something tells me you are not easily cast down." She gave him one quick, twinkling look and then said, "Good night, sir."

Jack chuckled and watched her disappear from view. The evening had passed off very well, he reflected. How much better it was to take his dinner with Cecily and Sir Waldo, for even if the old gentleman did talk rather too much, Jack had at least been able to have the pleasure of Cecily's company.

Of course, he did like and admire Sir Waldo. It was just that Jack was realizing he would be trading these more civilized meals for the privilege of having Cecily come to his room twice a day. That Cecily had suspected all along that he was, in truth, a gentleman, went a long way towards explaining her behaviour. He doubted that she would have been so accommodating if she had believed he was nothing more than a coachman. He flattered himself that she had enjoyed their private meetings almost as much as he had. His spirits soared at the thought, only to be damped by another. Cecily Wolverton was a lady, and a lady would take her charity seriously. If he had been a beggar with the smallpox, she would have attended him just as dutifully.

Still, Jack thought smiling to himself, now that she knew he was a gentleman he would have a better chance of impressing her with the Henley charm. Then, as he was passing in front of a mirror, he caught a glimpse of himself in the glass. The smile was wiped from his lips. What was he about? he asked himself. What right did he have to start a flirtation with a lady like Cecily Wolverton when he was nothing more than a coachman?

The clicking sound of a dog's nails echoed down the corridor, and Jack turned to find that Leto had risen from Sir Waldo's hearth to follow him to his room. He held out a hand for her to sniff and scratched her absently on the shoulder. Leto welcomed this attention with idiotic bliss and sat down on the floor to facilitate her enjoyment. Unable to refuse the invitation,

Jack lowered himself into a chair against the wall and continued petting her.

Like most dogs, Leto had an expression which could shift from complete idiocy to great sensitivity due to the soulful cast of her eyes. The fur about her eyes and muzzle was white, also, giving the appearance of wisdom gained through the years. Jack stared at her and then put one arm about her, happy to find such a trustworthy confident.

"You are a woman, Leto," he began. "What would you think of a fellow, without a claim to anything, who conducted himself in such a way as to engage the affections of a lady? Irresponsible, would you say? Reprehensible?"

Leto drew in her tongue and swallowed, shifting uncomfortably.

"Oh? As bad as that?" Jack frowned at her. "But what if he hadn't meant to? What if he couldn't help himself? What if he did it without thinking?"

Leto yawned with a whine and started to leave. Clearly, Jack was not behaving as he ought to. He called her back and started scratching her again where he knew she liked it best.

When she had settled back down, he confessed to her, "It's not so easy, you know, to remember *not* to enjoy someone's company too much. Especially when that person is pretty and friendly and always willing to enjoy a joke with the fellow." He was silent for a moment, thinking he might as easily have added that there was something else about her—maybe that air of authority mixed with just the right touch of femininity which he found so enchanting in such a small lady. So much more appealing than the usual coyness.

"Cecily Wolverton," he mused aloud. "Where have I heard that name before, Leto? You ought to be able to tell me." He looked at her reproachfully and got a lick on the hand. "Does she have other relatives? I have not heard her mention anyone besides her aunt. What about her parents? Are there sisters or brothers?" He paused. "You're not being much help!"

Leto looked at him blankly and he apologized to her with a pat upon the head.

"You might at least tell me why she does not go about. In the five weeks since I've been here, she's not had one social engagement. And I would swear that Sir Waldo is not the type to keep her here dancing attendance upon him."

He gave Leto one final pat and with the help of his crutch rose to his good foot. "Well, there's not much I'll learn about her from you, or by listening to your master's talk at dinner. I suppose the thing to do is catch Miss Cecily at breakfast and ask the fair lady myself. Always assuming I don't break my neck getting downstairs."

Leto looked up at him as if to make certain that he really had no intention of petting her further. Then with a sigh, she heaved herself up and walked slowly back down the corridor.

"No help," Jack said pensively to her retreating figure. "Absolutely no help at all."

THE NEXT DAY proved to be more fruitful, however, for when he hobbled into the breakfast parlour with the help of the footman, there was Cecily just sitting down to table. She was especially lovely this morning, he thought, dressed in a pretty sprigged muslin gown in bright green and yellow. She looked up in surprise, but a broad smile quickly lighted her face.

"Good morning, Mr. Henley!" she said. "I did not think to see you downstairs so soon. I trust this means you are mending well?"

Her greeting pleased Jack, for he could not doubt she was happy to see him. "If I am mending well, Miss Cecily, I am sure it is due to your excellent care," he answered. He did not intend to forgo this manner of address. In Sir Waldo's presence he would always address her as Miss Wolverton, but he would not give up the advantage he had already achieved.

Cecily directed a place to be set for him and he took his seat at the opposite end of the enormous table from her. The table dwarfed her tiny figure and she had to sit very erectly even to use her knife and fork to best advantage. After Jack was served, Cecily thanked the footman and dismissed him from the room, asking him to make himself available for Jack's return to his room.

Jack was delighted to watch this exchange. Cecily often had the air of a little girl playing at being grown up, but this was merely due to her size. He knew she was quite competent. If nothing else, the respect she received from the servants would have told him that, but Sir Waldo's manor showed the mark of a house well run. Sir Waldo himself could no longer be responsible for this efficiency, no matter what he had been in the past.

But there was something vaguely mysterious about her. Jack had noticed that she was treated with extraordinary deference for the granddaughter of a provincial baronet. It was almost as if she had been born to something better. There was a sense of command about her, a particular dignity, which made her the equal of any gentleman. There was nothing of the timid spinster helping to nurse the grandfather on whom she depended.

"Is this your home?" Jack ventured to ask her. "I mean, of course, is this where you live the better part of the year?"

An unexpected flush rose to her cheeks. "I suppose so . . . yes," answered Cecily uncertainly. "It was only two months ago—when you carried me here yourself—that I took up residence with my grandfather."

"And before that . . . ?"

"I was staying with my aunt near Shipston. You see," she explained, "It was just two years ago that my father, Lord Stourport, died. My mother has been gone some time longer."

"I am sorry," said Jack. Now he began to see. But the name Wolverton still puzzled him. "Sir Waldo was your mother's father then."

"No," Cecily corrected him quickly. There was something guarded in her manner, but she explained readily enough, "He is my father's father. *My* father, you see, assumed my mother's surname by Royal licence when he married her. She was baroness in her own right." Cecily went on to explain the unusual circumstances of her mother's inheritance. Then, she paused before adding, "The estate was unentailed."

A spark of intelligence stirred Jack's memory. So that was it. He remembered hearing about her father's death when he was in London. There was quite a bit of talk about it at the time—something about a missing will. But it did not concern him and he had paid it little attention. Before long other topics of conversation had come to take its place.

Cecily was regarding him with a peculiar look. In it was a measure of anxiety. He decided to be frank with her.

"Now that you have answered my question, I do remember something about your family," he admitted. "Your name was familiar, you see, but I did not recall where I had heard it. There was some puzzle surrounding your father's death, was there not? A missing document or something?"

She nodded. Jack noticed that she even seemed grateful for the chance to discuss it. "Yes. My father's will was never found. The estate my parents had amassed by the time of his death was considerable. And although I could not inherit the title specifically—after my mother it was with remainder 'to heirs general'—the large part of the estate was to have passed to me. My father had informed me of his intention, although there was never any doubt.

"But his will was never found. The courts supposed it had not been made, but I knew that it had.

His solicitors confirmed having drawn one up in my favour. I was to be co-heir to my cousin Alfred. But my father was a bit eccentric when it came to matters of business. He was mistrustful of agents and preferred to keep his papers in his own possession. The will ought to have been among his other documents, but was not."

Cecily related her misfortune in a calm, composed voice, which Jack found more touching than if she had offered him tears. There was hardly anything he could say, but one thought did occur to him.

He gave her an ironic grin. "Then it seems as if you and I have more than a little in common. We have both been dispossessed—you by an unfortunate chance, and I by my own folly."

Her expression, which had been rather serious, lightened at this, but she asked, "Is there no chance your father will forgive you? You were just a boy, after all."

Jack was startled by her words. His misdeeds had been committed only months ago, and yet, he realized, he had been just a boy. He no longer felt like one. The experience of having the responsibility of employment had done its job. He knew he had learned to be a man. This conviction caused him to respond cheerfully.

"Oh, I think he will. I am his only child, you see, and we have a great affection for each other. But he is a stern parent. Often I've wondered whether, if he had been somewhat less so, I, upon achieving the freedom of London, might have behaved..." He broke off.

"But that is not important. I trust that he, at some point, will look at me and see that I have undergone a *material conversion* to his point of view."

Jack finished his speech in such an amusing fashion that Cecily had to smile. They talked about his coaching experiences and Jack told her more of the things that had happened to him, this time not fearful of giving himself away. There had been times on the box when he would dearly have loved to laugh about one of his passengers, but he had not dared. Now it was a great relief to be able to do so.

He told her of one such occasion, when a particularly belligerent woman had insisted upon displacing a passenger on the rear seat, because, she said, she found his face offensive.

"She rather reminds me of the red-faced woman who did not like you to take me up, the day I rode with you," said Cecily laughing. "But I suppose someone always complains when you take up an extra passenger."

Jack's eyes gleamed. He regarded her fixedly. "Oh, but I haven't. You were the only one." He took the last bite of his breakfast, all the while watching and waiting for his words to sink in.

Cecily took only a few seconds to recognize the compliment, but when she did she looked away hastily. He could detect the quiver of a smile at the corner of her lips.

"Then I must thank you again," she said breathlessly. "It was fortunate for me you were the driver that day. I was quite anxious to get to my grandfather."

Jack inwardly admonished himself for resuming the flirtation he had intended to renounce. Then he realized that she was about to tell him what he had always wanted to know.

Cecily's eyes had flickered up to his and then away again. "You must have thought it strange for a lady to be riding alone on the mail. My grandfather made it plain to you that he did not approve of it. In fact, however, it had something to do with the topic we were just discussing. My cousin Alfred, you see, the present Lord Stourport—" she could not prevent an unaccustomed wryness from creeping into her voice "—had written me his intention of visiting the same day. I thought if I could take the mail, my aunt would be able to say I had missed receiving his message. There was no other means of getting away at my disposal. I hastened down to the village in time to catch the mail, but was disappointed by the man in the booking office. I was rather desperate at the time, otherwise I would not have attempted to bribe you." Cecily looked up at him from beneath her lashes; her eyes held a sparkle. That memory was particularly entertaining to them both.

Jack laughed aloud. "I do not hold that against you, Miss Cecily. My honour goes undiminished, as does yours." He said nothing about her reasons for fleeing, however.

"Thank you, Mr. Henley," she said pertly.

Jack smiled at her engagingly. "Would you not call me Jack?" he asked. "After all, I have been calling you Cecily these many weeks and you have not stopped me." He had anticipated that she would be discomposed as indeed she was. Still, he did not see any harm in the suggestion. He very much wanted to be her friend.

"All right. I shall call you Jack," she said. Shyness, not normally a part of her character, threatened to overcome her. She rose from the table and asked him if he would like her to call the footman.

Jack would rather not have ended their conversation so quickly, but he obliged her by accepting that the meal was now over. He trusted there would soon be another time when he could talk to her alone. Jack was finding it more and more difficult to deny his desire for a flirtation with Cecily, and the temptation to pursue her was proving to be more than he could resist.

CHAPTER EIGHT

CECILY HAD BEEN SURPRISED to see Jack down that morning for breakfast and equally surprised to find herself confiding in him. But the day held more than one unexpected event for her, for before noon a visitor arrived. She was finishing a complete turnout of one of the guest bedrooms, when a servant came running to inform her that Lord Stourport was downstairs asking to see her.

She received the news in a way that gave the maid no doubt as to her feelings upon the subject. "The devil!" she cried with exasperation. Then recalling to whom she was speaking, she tried to mask her irritation, instructing the girl to show Lord Stourport into the parlour. "You may tell my cousin," she added, "that I shall be down within the hour. I shall have to freshen myself."

Cecily took her time washing and dressing again, hoping that Alfred would take the hint and not expect to be asked to dinner. His arrival had startled her. He was not, after all, any kin to Sir Waldo, and until this visit had never set foot in her grandfather's house. She remembered the peculiar tone of his last letter. This time he had not sent word before calling on her. Had he been more careful, meaning not to give her a chance to slip away? What did he want?

When Cecily finally joined her cousin Alfred in the parlour, she greeted him with cool civility. He took her hand and bowed over it with exaggerated courtesy, then held it while looking her over with his heavily lidded eyes.

"A charming gown, my dear Cecily," he said. "And you look charmingly in it. It quite becomes you."

Cecily could not return the compliment, for Alfred did not look at all well. His complexion was a sickly shade of white, he was not well shaved, and his neck-cloth was imperfectly pressed. Indeed, his appearance came as something of a shock to her, for Alfred had always been rather a dandy. Any sign of neglect in his toilet was certain to mean he was feeling poorly.

"Won't you be seated, Alfred," she said, more kindly than she had intended. "You have quite surprised me by your visit. I hope nothing is wrong at Stourport?"

Alfred's eyes glinted sharply for a moment, but he took the chair she offered him and replied languidly, "You have nothing to fear on that account, my dear Cecily. All is well. I have made some slight changes among the servants which I hope will not distress you, but I found my Uncle Stephen's people to be somewhat lacking . . . in the proper polish, one might say. I am afraid I could not leave things quite as they were. I hope you are not offended." He said this last with an ingratiating air which Cecily did not trust.

She managed to answer him with tolerable calm, although his implications angered her. "Stourport is yours now, Alfred. How could I be offended by any changes you might care to make?"

Well Cecily knew the excellence of her father's servants, but she also knew they had no desire to work for the new baron. Several of them had informed her of their intention of seeking new situations as soon as she should be gone. In fact, she had written several letters of recommendation on their behalf.

Her answer seemed to satisfy Alfred, though, for he gave her a feline grin.

"But you have not told me the purpose of your call," Cecily reminded him. "Or are you just stopping on your way somewhere else?"

Alfred responded with a wounded air. "It is you I have come to see, Cousin. Can you doubt it? Did your aunt not tell you that I wrote of my intention to visit, more than a month ago? Imagine my hurt when I discovered you had just left her house on the very day of my arrival."

There was a glimmer of suspicion in his eyes, and Cecily wondered if Alfred had discovered her means of evading him. "Yes, she did inform me, by post after I arrived here. But my plans were already made, you see. I am sorry you were inconvenienced."

Alfred beamed upon her. "So considerate, my dear Cecily. But then you always were a model of feminine virtue."

Cecily laughed. "My grandfather would smile to hear you say so, Alfred, remembering my childhood scrapes. I was not such a pattern card then, if you recall. Either your memory is at fault or you must be trying to gammon me!"

His smile stiffened. He seemed more than usually on edge, shifting back and forth quickly from amusement to irritation. "You must not deprecate yourself, Cecily. It does not become you."

She sighed inwardly. It appeared that Alfred was not going to volunteer the purpose of his visit and that she would have to drag it from him.

"Are there business matters you wish to discuss with me, Alfred?"

He started, and then waved an impatient hand. "Did I not just say that it is you I have come to see, Cecily? I am here to help you. As soon as I found out where you were—your aunt, you must know, gave me to understand that you had gone visiting, and I did not know your whereabouts. Anyway, as soon as I knew them, I hurried to be with you."

Cecily looked at him blankly. He explained. "Your poor grandpapa," he said in a mournful tone. "To think that you have been down here nursing him, at his bedside as it were, without the support and comfort of another family member nearby.... Why, it is most distressing!"

A moment's pause, and Cecily laughed. Alfred's eyes narrowed unpleasantly. "You must forgive me, Cousin," she said, "But I had no idea you were under such a misapprehension. I am here by my grandfather's invitation and by my choice. We get on quite well together, I assure you, and he is not in such a bad way that I feel myself the least burdened. I have been enjoying myself immensely. So you see, there is not the slightest need for you to trouble yourself."

But Alfred, it seemed, would not believe her. "You are too noble, Cousin. I cannot depend on you to be truthful in this circumstance, for I perceive you are trying not to impose upon my kindness. You see, I know you too well. I insist upon being allowed to help you. I will have my things taken to my room, if you please, if you will be kind enough to ask the housekeeper just where I should establish myself for the present."

Cecily looked at him in horror. "You do not mean you intend to stay, Alfred!"

He smiled as though she had intended this as a compliment to him. "Yes, of course. You may indeed be surprised by the degree of my cousinly devotion, but I beg you to consult your own heart on the matter to see whether I might not have another interest in mind. For the present, however, I shall say nothing more on the subject. Will you have the goodness to have that woman—Mrs. Shelby, is it—show me to my room? I find myself desperately in need of a rest."

Cecily could not deny such a pointed request. Little as she trusted Alfred, and wanting him there even less, she could see that he indeed needed a rest. "It is Mrs. *Selby*," she corrected him. "And I shall ring for her."

In a few moments Mrs. Selby had come and, with a poor show of grace, had taken Alfred to his room. Cecily sat for a while longer, gazing at nothing in particular and wearing a frown. Alfred's visit was a puzzle to her. She could not credit his motives. Had he not already taken all that should have been hers? She had nothing left to give him.

A scraping sound in the corridor awoke her from her thoughts, and she looked up to see Jack standing in the doorway. Of its own accord, a bright smile sprang to her lips.

"Am I disturbing you, Cecily?" he asked. She did not have to answer for her smile told it all.

He hobbled into the room in response to her invitation, and she had the opportunity to watch. She could not help contrasting Jack's splendid figure with Alfred's weaker frame. In spite of his having to hobble on one crutch—perhaps even because of it—his firm muscles drew her attention. But he could not be aware of it, for his blue eyes met hers and sparkled with humour.

"I make quite a sight, I suppose, stumbling into your parlour. Not the sort of guest one's accustomed to."

Cecily could not very well confess what she had been thinking, so she assured him it was of no consequence. He took a seat beside her and heaved a sigh of relief.

"I must say," he began, "no amount of long hours on the box could make me quite so eager to arrive at my destination as this crutch does. It is a most inferior form of travel."

Cecily smiled at his pleasantry, but could not give him her full attention. Her mind was distracted by the knowledge that Alfred was in the house and by her need to know his purpose.

Jack must have realized that something was bothering her, for he stared at her silently for a moment before saying, "The servants have just informed me that your cousin, Lord Stourport, has come for a visit. Is that what has you so blue-deviled?"

She started to deny it, but faced with the intense concern in his expression, could not. "Yes," she admitted finally. "I cannot help but wonder what he's up to. You see, he's never been here before, and cannot have a legitimate reason for coming."

"What does he say?"

"That he's come to *help* me," said Cecily in an oozing voice.

Jack laughed. "And that won't wash? Well, I suppose you know your cousin better than I, so I'll take your word for it. What do you suppose his true reasons are?"

Cecily's frown redescended. "I do not know. Charity, familial or otherwise, is not in Alfred's line, so I cannot think he has come to assist me. And he cannot possibly have run through my father's estate in just six months, so I doubt he is here for money. That does not leave much upon which to speculate." Then she added, "But I do know that there is something he wants of me."

Jack's smile had faded, too. "He sounds a pretty fellow. Is there nothing you can do to avoid him? Why not send him about his business?"

"I ought to, I suppose," agreed Cecily. "But that would take a degree of incivility I am not used to employing. And besides, I tried that once before and only succeeded in delaying his visit. I must find out at some point what scheme he has in mind."

Her companion nodded. "Well," he said, "I admire you for bearding the lion in his den. Just remember, however, that I am here and willing to be of assistance whenever you should need it." He smiled reassuringly and Cecily felt a glow of unaccustomed warmth. She suddenly realized how much more confident she felt facing Alfred because Jack was in the house. Once again, she had confided in him without reflecting on the wisdom of it, and without a thought of discretion.

"Thank you," she said rising, not wishing to burden him further. "Now I shall have to go inform my grandfather that there is an uninvited guest staying under his roof. He will not like to hear that it is Alfred, so it will take some skill on my part to avoid alarming him. Will you visit him afterwards and help to entertain him?"

"I would be delighted to," agreed Jack, rising quickly to his good leg. "But this evening... shall we be dining in his room, or..."

Cecily paused. "I had not thought of that," she said. Then she sighed. "No. At least, *I* cannot. I shall have to entertain Alfred downstairs."

"Then I shall come down, too," said Jack quickly.

Cecily gave a smile of relief and then noticed his clothes. She could not help but laugh. "I cannot wait to see Alfred's face when he learns that he is to dine with a coachman. My cousin," she explained, "is not the broadest in his views."

Jack's eyes lit with mischief. "Then it shall be my pleasure to enlighten him," he said.

Cecily went off to her grandfather's room with a lighter heart, and her confident mood was of great help in convincing Sir Waldo that he had nothing about which to worry. She told him that she and Jack would have to dine without him that evening, and she managed to amuse him with the picture Alfred and Jack would make at the table together.

When she had done, Sir Waldo sighed and patted her hand. "I cannot like it, Cecily. What the blazes does the fellow mean, coming here like this? If Jack weren't here to lend his presence, I should have the fellow thrown out—Lord Stourport or not!"

Cecily hastened to comfort him, but her cheeks were suddenly filled with warmth. "Indeed you should, but as you say, with Jack here there is no need. I shall have sufficient company so that Alfred cannot pass off any of his tricks on me. Jack has already assured me of his wish to be helpful." She spoke these last words self-consciously,

Her grandfather looked at her sharply. "In your confidence, is he? Good. I like the young man. If I were young and fit as he is, I'd . . ." He did not finish his sentence, but his shrewd eyes took in Cecily's confusion with a gleam of contentment.

A LITTLE WHILE LATER, Jack was shown into the room. Cecily had departed in order to see that dinner would be ordered for three persons downstairs.

Sir Waldo looked him over with a thorough scrutiny, while Jack waited for him to speak. This went on for some minutes, before the younger man showed signs of amusement at this treatment and directed an enquiring look at Sir Waldo.

It recalled the old man to the present. "Jack, my boy," he said, and his eyes held a spark of excitement. "There is something I have to tell you."

As Jack listened earnestly, Sir Waldo recounted to him the circumstances surrounding his son's missing will. Then, with only a slight pause he continued, "Now what I am about to say to you must remain strictly between us. You know that I'm as good as a cripple. Been lying here stiff as a board for nigh on two years with little to amuse me but Leto here—" he gave her a pat "—and Selby's sour face. I've got my books, but I know 'em by heart so there's nothing new in that. Cecily's my only joy."

Jack watched him silently, his heart giving a sudden leap.

Sir Waldo continued, staring grimly into his eyes. "If there is anything I won't stand for, it is for her to be harmed in any way."

Jack returned his stare, letting his silence speak for itself.

After a while, seemingly satisfied with his response, Sir Waldo reverted to his former manner and said excitedly, "I've done quite a lot of thinking while

I've been lying here. And it seems to me there's just one possibility." He paused. "Alfred must have done away with the will."

"Have you any proof?" Jack asked him quickly.

Sighing, the old man shook his head. "No, but I'd swear to it." He explained his reasons for thinking Cecily's father never intended to leave her homeless, adding, "And who stood to benefit by it all if not Alfred? He took all she had. And except for a few words of regret at the start of the legal proceedings, he's done nothing to make it up to her. Not a penny's allowance in all this time. But it's *how* he did it that I can't make out."

"Was the possibility looked into at the time?"

Sir Waldo snorted. "Barely. They wouldn't want to offend the new lord then, would they? All they could reasonably do was search the premises, ask the servants a few questions. Alfred's smarter than that. If he did do away with it, you can be sure it was nowhere the solicitors could find it.

"And what's he here for now? There is no reason for Alfred to have any more to do with Cecily. None whatsoever. The only interest he could possibly have in her at this point would be if the will were somehow found. Then, of course, he would have much to lose. But if that's a possibility, then he must not have it himself for he would most certainly destroy it, and I refuse to believe he did not have something to do with its disappearance!"

Jack was frowning. "From what both you and Miss Wolverton have to say about him, he seems a likely suspect. It puzzles me that your son did not take greater steps to exclude him from the inheritance."

Sir Waldo snorted. "Stephen had his odd ways. I'm sure he thought he had taken care of everything in his will and that it was safe. Alfred's father was just such an unsavoury fellow, you see. To my mind that's why the patent was written so as to pass the title to Cecily's mother. *Her* father was trying to keep it from passing to his younger brother's family."

"Well, it is certainly a mystery," agreed Jack, shaking his head. "Thank you for your confidence, Sir Waldo. I assure you it has been well placed. I doubt that I could find anything to confirm your suspicions, but if anything occurs to me, I will notify you directly. Meanwhile, do not fear for Ce—Miss Wolverton," he amended quickly. "I will take care she is not bothered by her cousin while he is here."

"Good lad!" said Sir Waldo. He had not missed Jack's slip of the tongue, but found nothing to censure in it. If the boy were taken with his granddaughter, so much the better. He hated to think of Cecily all alone when he would be gone, but he could do little to play at matchmaker. Now, it seemed, he had been landed the perfect choice, by an accident of the Royal Mail. He just hoped Cecily would agree with him. Surely there had been a strange bit of colour in her cheeks today. And Jack: would he really be willing—or able—to help his granddaughter out of this bumblebroth?

CHAPTER NINE

NOW JACK HAD several reasons to attend dinner downstairs with Cecily and her cousin Alfred. At precisely the appointed hour, dressed as a coachman, he made his way to the dining room. The servants were now used to his mode of dressing, and found nothing strange to say about it. Mr. Selby could not think it proper, it was true. But his clothes notwithstanding, Mr. Selby had to admit the young gentleman's presence had caused a favourable improvement in Sir Waldo's spirits of late. Mrs. Selby, too, had noticed some recent changes in her mistress's behaviour. She was more likely to sing while she worked. So, even if they had their own objections to the young man—he was, after all, not quite what one was used to—they kept them to themselves. And when they pitted him against Lord Stourport...well, there was nothing more to be said.

When Jack entered the dining room, it was to find Alfred waiting impatiently. He was dressed in the extreme of Town fashion. His evening coat was blue and double-breasted, and bore a double row of large brass buttons. His breeches were elegantly tied at the knees, and his stockings were spotlessly white. As Jack entered, Alfred let out a slight cry and raised a quizzing glass to his eye.

"My good fellow," he drawled. "You have obviously mistaken your entrance. The kitchen is round the back."

"You must apologize to my guest, Alfred." Cecily's voice came quickly from the doorway. She had arrived shortly after Jack's entry and was in time to hear Alfred's comment. She presented Jack to her cousin, and he made a slight bow.

Cecily herself had decided not to dress elaborately for the evening. She would rather, she had decided, appear to disadvantage than make Jack feel more uncomfortable because of his clothes. Therefore, she was wearing a plain white muslin gown, suitable for evening, but without any adornment. A fringed tunic in brown silk protected her from the chill.

"Your guest?" enquired Alfred, still quizzing Jack with his glass. His examination transferred to Cecily and took in the simplicity of her costume. "How novel, my dear Cecily. Since when has it become fashionable for one to invite common labourers to one's dinner parties?"

Cecily's eyes sparked in anger, but Jack calmed her with a good-humoured glance. "You are mistaken, Alfred," she said through clenched teeth. "Mr. Henley is the only son of Sir Geoffrey Henley."

Alfred was unabashed. "May I suggest then, my good fellow," he said maliciously, "that you find a new tailor?"

Here Jack, seeing that Cecily had grown speechless with anger, stepped into the breach.

"You will naturally find my dress queer for the occasion," he allowed. "But you see, I had a coaching accident, and my limb is so swollen that my own breeches will not fit over it."

"Then you had much better have some made to the purpose," said Alfred. "I, for one, should never think of appearing in public in such togs. One could easily mistake you for the coachman! I'm certain *I* did."

There was a moment's silence in the room. Jack, despite his intention to remain in good humour, could find no answer to this slur. If Cecily had not been there, he would gladly have admitted to being a coachman and challenged Alfred for his offensive remarks. But Jack perceived suddenly what an embarrassment it would be for Cecily for any of her family or friends to know that she had dined with a mail coachman. He swallowed the retort that sprang to his lips.

Cecily, for her part, was only bothered by Alfred's lack of manners, and was unwilling to expose Jack to it any longer than necessary. She begged them to take their places for dinner, and hastily changed the subject.

But it was not long before Alfred had turned the conversation back to Jack. He had been observing Jack and Cecily through narrowed eyes, and had not missed the smiles exchanged between them. That he was disturbed by Jack's presence was evident.

"I do not believe you told me, Cousin, just how your injured friend came to be here." Turning to Jack, he asked, "Were you visiting Sir Waldo when the accident occurred, or had you other business?"

Jack gave him a direct look. "Neither," he said. "I was riding through town on the mail when the axle broke. Sir Waldo and Miss Wolverton were kind enough to take me in until my leg should heal."

Alfred raised his quizzing glass again and regarded Cecily. "How noble of you, Cousin, to take in a complete stranger off the mail. He might have been anybody. I have often observed that the most peculiar mixture of humanity travels upon it. I have never had the pleasure myself, you understand. I really could not relish the thought of being at such close quarters with persons of questionable background."

"Really, Alfred?" observed Cecily with great pleasure. "*I* had reason to take the mail quite recently and found it a delightful experience. You must try it sometime. It will do you a world of good." She exchanged a secret glance with Jack, whose eyes danced warmly back at her.

Alfred was not pleased with her quick defence of her guest. "You must count yourself fortunate, Mr. Henley, for I observe you have been as well received as I was myself. And I, of course, am a blood relative."

Cecily flushed uncomfortably. Alfred's remarks had been made with just enough malice to encourage her to feel guilt. "Mr. Henley and Sir Waldo share an interest in coaching, Alfred. He has been kind enough to sit with my grandfather on many occasions."

As soon as the words were out of her mouth, she regretted having spoken them. Alfred smiled disagreeably.

"You must let me visit your grandpapa's room, Cecily. I shall be happy to entertain him."

"Oh, no!" Cecily protested. Then as Alfred's eyes narrowed dangerously, she amended, "That is, I don't like to put you to the trouble, though your offer is very kind. Sir Waldo is rather particular in his interests and as much as he is an old dear, he can be rather difficult. He especially enjoys discussing coaching and Jack indulges him by the hour. However, I doubt whether stories about Town would entertain him quite so well. He never was one to enjoy the Season, you know, and I shouldn't like you to feel at a loss."

Alfred's smile turned into an expression of distaste. "It never ceases to amaze me, this fascination with pedestrian trades and common sports. One would think the Romans had all been coachmen the way the drivers are catered to. And the rest of the rabble—cockfighters, boxers and the like—it is more than I can fathom. You, sir," he said to Jack, "perhaps you can explain it to me if you are a sportsman."

Jack would not take offense. He smiled graciously. "I can well understand that a passion for sports would be inexplicable to you," he said by way of reply.

Alfred smiled tightly, but remained unruffled. "I will accept that as a compliment," he said. "I cannot think it worthy of the dignity of a peer to be found engaging in such lowly pursuits."

"Perhaps not," conceded Jack. "Nevertheless, most of them are. Likely one has to be born to it."

This veiled reference to Alfred's recent accession was clearly provoking, but Cecily stepped in before her cousin could respond.

"You do not look well, Alfred," she said. "I noticed it this afternoon when you arrived. I hope you will get the sleep you require while you are here."

Alfred allowed Jack's remark to drop as a more pressing matter occurred to him. "Thank you, Cousin. I shall. But I must ask you to have your grandfather's man—Shelby, isn't it—tend to me while I am here."

Cecily looked at him in amazement. "Why Alfred! You do not mean to say you have not brought Sudbury with you!"

Alfred blanched visibly as she said the name. "No. I have not," he said shortly. "I had to turn him off. He proved to be the most unsatisfactory of servants. You see," he added, attempting once again to ingratiate himself with his cousin, "it was not only your father's servants with whom I have had to be firm."

"But Sudbury?" Cecily persisted. "I thought he was essential to your happiness. Why, after the praise I have heard you heap upon him countless times, I cannot imagine your finding fault with him."

Alfred looked at her coldly. "Then I shall simply say I was deceived in him." He shuddered slightly. "If you have quite finished now, I had rather not pass the remainder of the meal in discussions about my personal servants. Mr. Henley will surely not be amused."

Cecily pretended not to take his intended slur on Jack's questionable mode of dress. "I am terribly sorry, Alfred, but I cannot ask Selby to attend to you. He is occupied quite enough with my grandfather. The best I shall be able to do is to ask one of the footmen to assist you."

Her cousin looked put out. "Then I shall have to shave myself? Certainly your Selby fellow could spare me the time for that much?"

Cecily shook her head with an exaggerated show of regret. "I'm afraid not. Selby is also at Mr. Henley's disposal, so he really cannot be expected to do more."

Alfred's pride was clearly offended. He vented his spleen by lifting his quizzing glass to his eye once again and examining Jack thoroughly. The object of his regard was not discomposed. "On that account, perhaps I would do well to dispense with his services."

Cecily had not quite finished her meal, but she rose at that remark. "I shall be having tea in the drawing room if you care to join me after your port. Mr. Henley?"

Jack rose, also, and made his bow to Alfred. "You will excuse me, I hope, Lord Stourport. With this leg of mine I dare not dip too deeply. I will join Miss Wolverton directly."

Alfred stared back and forth between them for a moment and then smiled disagreeably. "Of course, dear fellow. Although I will admit I had rather looked forward to a little manly chat. If you have not the stomach for it, however, I quite understand. I shall not tarry." He made this last promise to Cecily, who offered her arm to Jack. The two of them passed slowly from the room.

"Phew!" said Jack, once they were out of earshot. "He is a poisonous creature. I can certainly credit Sir Waldo's suspicions of him."

Cecily turned to him in surprise. Jack looked at her apologetically. "Your grandfather confided his thinking to me this afternoon. I hope you do not object. He is quite worried about you, you know, and he cannot do anything to help in his present condition. I believe it was a comfort to him to know I would be watching out for you."

Cecily flushed but he could see she was not really displeased. "No. I do not mind," she said after a moment's hesitation. "And if, by his suspicions, you mean the theft of my father's will . . ."

Jack nodded.

"Then," she continued, looking at him directly, "I suppose I share them, although my grandfather and I have never spoken of it. I've often wondered if the notion had occurred to him.

"And I would gladly have told you myself if I did not fear dragging you into our private family matters. They do not concern you, and you must not feel under any obligation to take an interest in them."

Jack frowned. "I believe Sir Waldo realizes I am more than simply in his debt."

Cecily hastened to amend what she had said. "Of course. Sir Waldo thinks of you as a guest in his house. He has taken to you considerably. It is just," she said, lowering her eyes, "that you will have to resume your employment once your leg has healed. You will have no time to investigate the matter, even if you were kind enough to wish to do so."

Jack was silent. What she said was true. His leg was healing. Another week, perhaps two, and he would have to return to his driving—if the mail would have him. He stifled a sigh. He had to admit he had no desire to take it up again.

But Cecily interrupted his thoughtful silence. "In any case," she said, "there is little anyone can do. Unless the will is found, things will have to remain as they are."

Putting aside his own troubles for the moment, Jack asked, "Could it really be possible that your cousin made off with it? Was he in the house when your father died?"

Cecily nodded. "Yes, indeed. My father was ill for about a week before he died. Realizing that he might not live much longer, and knowing Alfred to be his titular heir, I thought it best that I should inform my cousin of his illness. Alfred posted down with Sudbury immediately, and was there when he died. But I could have sworn that Alfred did not go near my father's library. It was not locked, mind you. We had no reason to think there was a need for it. It is just that Alfred spent the majority of his time inside my father's room when he was not attending to his own daily needs. I remember being quite put out that he did not allow me sufficient time alone with my father. But he did offer to sit with him whenever I had to leave the room, and I could only be grateful. Grandpapa ought not to have mentioned his suspicions to you, and I should not indulge in them myself."

"And yet, you do not want him to visit your grandfather?"

Cecily smiled sadly. "My father was unconscious and could not really know who was with him. Grandpapa would sooner die of apoplexy than let Alfred cross the threshold."

Jack raised his brows significantly, showing that he understood her meaning, but then looked thoughtful. "I can see that proving his guilt would be quite difficult. If no one saw him enter your father's library, then there is little to go on."

Cecily shook her head. "There is really nothing. We ought not to be speaking of it. The servants were questioned thoroughly by my father's solicitor, but none of them could attest to having seen him anywhere in the vicinity of the library. And they all would have been happy to do so," she said wryly.

Jack chuckled. "He's already my favourite candidate for a villain, and I've just now met him."

He was happy to see that her spirits had risen while they talked, despite the unhappy topic. "If I had a glass before me," he ventured, "I would make a toast to the day when both our fortunes are restored. But a cup of tea will have to do, I suppose."

They had reached the drawing room by now and found the tea tray waiting for them. Cecily poured them each a cup and they raised them in mock salute. Then she smiled, as their eyes met.

"We *have* both experienced rather odd twists of fate, have we not?" she said comfortably.

Jack nodded. "I don't know how my father would take to being described as such, but I perfectly agree with you," he said.

Cecily gave a gurgle of laughter. "Is he a very proud man then, your father?"

"No more than he ought to be," said Jack. "He is the first baronet, you see, and he does not intend to be the last."

A flicker of empathy crossed her face. "He sounds as if he might be very like my other grandfather, General Wolverton. Mama always said it was the creation of his peerage that had meant the most to him. He was disappointed not to have sons, and then again when there were no grandsons."

"Sir Waldo does not seem to mind," said Jack with a twinkle.

"No," agreed Cecily, laughing and shaking her head. "As soon as Sir Waldo found I could handle a carriage-and-four, he became quite reconciled to having a granddaughter."

Jack's eyes gleamed. "I should think he would. When I am better, perhaps you would ride out with me in the carriage and show me how well you handle the reins."

"Certainly, sir," she said, meeting the challenge. "How soon do you think you will be ready?"

Jack shrugged. "My leg feels much better," he said. "Perhaps the doctor would give me permission to put my weight on it now. I do not think I should drive until I have had a chance to walk."

"I shall send for him in the morning," said Cecily. "If he agrees, you could take a turn or two about the garden in the afternoons."

"Will you accompany me?" asked Jack. She flushed, but nodded.

"I do not think you ought to go by yourself. You might tire and need someone to go back to fetch a servant."

Jack agreed with his gravest demeanour. "Oh, no. I must not be allowed to go alone. Think of all the horrible things that might happen to me. I should be much too fearful. But knowing you are there to assist me should make the effort reasonably tolerable."

Cecily looked at him teasingly. "But I shall have no more of your tricks. I will not be such a slowtop as to fall for them again."

"You are quite correct," Jack said, "and I do make my apologies for such a subterfuge." He smiled engagingly and added, "I trust you did not mind too terribly much?"

Cecily flushed at his obvious meaning. "I cannot deny that your antics were amusing, but had you told me the truth from the outset, there would have been no need for them."

Jack sensed her slight censure and his tone became suddenly earnest. "You do see though, don't you, why I could not say who I was?" he asked.

Cecily frowned slightly. "I think so," she said slowly. And then, "Perhaps you have a measure of your father's pride."

Jack was taken aback. "Pride? It was nothing of the sort. But how could I claim to be Sir Geoffrey's son if he would not claim me himself? For that matter, why should you have believed me?"

Cecily could not answer, and something occurred to Jack which provoked him to say, "If you had not lost your fortune, I doubt very much you would be sharing the same pot of tea right now with a disinherited son of a baronet."

"That is true," agreed Cecily. Then she noticed how serious he had become and added quickly, "But only if you mean I might not have been here at the time. Otherwise, it could make no difference."

But Jack shook his head and gave her a slight smile. "Perhaps not to you. But I doubt I would be imposing myself on an heiress. Besides, you would be fully occupied with social engagements, and would have little time to entertain a coachman."

Cecily denied it stubbornly, declaring, "There is no use in imagining it any other way, whatever you say. Our separate quirks of fate *have* landed us both here, and I am very grateful, if for no other reason than I find you quite useful in helping me to avoid Alfred."

The playfulness in her manner cheered him, and he dismissed his unwelcome thoughts. Then, inclining his head at the dubious compliment she had paid him, he responded in kind, "I will engage to be useful in that respect, Mistress Cecily—or any other—whenever I shall be wanted."

CHAPTER TEN

BUT, THE NEXT MORNING, Jack was not as useful in keeping Alfred at bay as Cecily would have liked. The doctor had been called in to see him right after breakfast, and Cecily had stayed downstairs to write letters. She had not worried that Alfred would disturb her, for he was known to stay abed mornings. She was not happy, therefore, to hear his voice from the doorway wishing her a soft "good morning."

She looked up quickly from her work and greeted him coolly. "Good morning, Alfred. I trust you slept well. You have only to ring and breakfast will be brought to you in the breakfast parlour." She had hoped by this suggestion to discourage him from bothering her, but was disappointed.

He entered smiling. "That can wait, my dear Cecily. I am delighted to find you alone. Your other guest quite monopolizes you." She made no doubt that Alfred referred to the night before, when she had been quite content to share the drawing room with Jack but had made their excuses as soon as Alfred made his entrance.

Cecily kept her composure. "Mr. Henley is injured and is in need of my assistance, Alfred."

"Exactly so," he said. "But I hope you will not blame me if I had hoped for a little of that attention myself. After all, what can the company of a fellow who dresses like a servant be to you, Cecily? You were born to better things."

This was more than she could quite tolerate and she retorted, "Who better to know that than you, Alfred! Do you not occupy the house I was to inherit?"

She regretted her harsh words as soon as they were spoken for her cousin merely smiled as though she had offered him the perfect chance to speak. "I hope, dear Cousin, that you do not blame me for what transpired. I assure you, I was as astonished by my cousin Stephen's change of heart as you were. But I can only regard it as that, a change of heart. Perhaps he realized the extreme illogic of passing on a title to me, with no estate to support it."

"Leaving me with no provision whatsoever? I cannot think that was his intention."

Alfred shrugged. "As to that, dear Cousin, you would be the best one to judge. Perhaps he thought you would be more distressed to learn of his change of heart in writing."

Cecily was barely able to control her wrath. "Are you suggesting that my father deliberately destroyed his own will?"

"My dear Cecily. I should not suggest anything so distressing. But let us not go over the past. I have come to discuss your future."

"My future!" cried Cecily, not a little alarmed. "Whatever can you mean, Alfred?"

He smiled coyly. "Come now, Cecily. Surely your feminine instincts will have told you why I am here! You cannot—certainly not after receiving my last missive to you—be doubtful of my meaning."

Cecily's heart beat strangely. She had the most urgent desire to flee the room. "You are mistaken, Cousin. I am completely at a loss."

Alfred laughed mirthlessly. "What a coquette you are, Cecily! I had not thought it. You must know that it is my intention to lay my heart at your feet. I offer you marriage."

The proposal was made without the slightest effort to appear impassioned, and for that Cecily could only be grateful. She swallowed her retort and answered him with all the civility she could muster, "I thank you, Alfred, for your kind offer. But we should not suit."

He was clearly astonished by her refusal. "But, Cousin! Only think! I offer you a return to your father's home...security! What could you possibly wish that I cannot give you?"

Cecily coloured in anger. "There *is* the small matter of affection and respect between husband and wife, Alfred. Again, I thank you for the compliment you have paid me, but I cannot accept."

Alfred smiled confidently. "Is that what is troubling you? Then I must have expressed myself badly. But since we have been intimate so long I thought that declarations of love were not necessary. Let me assure you, Cousin, that I ardently love and respect you. In time, I am sure you will grow to regard me with the same degree of affection."

This was too much. Cecily could only be offended by his attempt to gammon her, for she knew he felt none of the emotions he was professing.

She rose from her writing desk, which she had not left during this exchange and, straightening her shoulders, made as if to leave. "You have had my answer, Alfred. I should be sorry to say something which might wound you."

Suddenly, Alfred's countenance betrayed an unpleasantness from which Cecily shrank instinctively.

He reached for her arm as she tried to pass him and held her against her will. Standing so close to him, Cecily could see that his eyes were shot through with red veins, as if he had not slept. "I suggest you think over my proposal, dear Cecily," he said through clenched teeth. "Your prospects are not so promising without a fortune to go along with that pretty face."

Cecily's heart contracted with fear. What Alfred said was true. But his manner was so desperate as to frighten her. "Are you threatening me, Alfred?" she asked with all the composure at her command.

He released her at once and inclined his head with an air of apology, drawing his heavy lids over his eyes. "Forgive me if I have offended you. I meant only to point out that my proposal, upon reflection, might become more attractive to you. It is not every day that one is given an opportunity to right a situation which, despite a lack of any requirement on my part to do so, would give me great pleasure to correct."

Cecily forced her rapid breathing to subside. "In that case, I will certainly think about your proposal. Now, if you will excuse me..."

He stepped aside and allowed her to pass from the room. Feeling suddenly that staying in the same house with Alfred was more than she could bear, Cecily made quickly for the garden to compose herself under the shelter of its trees. She strolled about for some time, thinking over what had just occurred, and chiefly wondering what Alfred intended.

What could have possessed him to offer for her? She was under no illusions as to his affection for her. In fact, she was inclined to suspect that he had as severe a dislike for her as she had for him. Then why had she told him she would think over his offer? Did the truth of his assertions frighten her to the extent that she would consider marriage to Alfred?

Cecily shuddered. The thought was more revolting than any she could imagine. Better to spend her life in lonely spinsterhood than to consider spending it with Alfred.

At that moment, she rounded the corner of a hedge and saw a figure approaching. Her heart bounded with relief when she perceived it was Jack. His straight, strong figure gave her a strange feeling of reassurance. Smiling, she hastened to meet him, barely resisting the absurd temptation to run.

"Does this mean the doctor will allow you to go for walks?" she asked him after they had greeted one another.

He nodded cheerfully. "It does. He said I might put my weight on the broken limb, so long as I take care not to fall and do not try any tricks. I assured him nothing could be further from my mind." Then he added in a perplexed tone, "He seemed to have his suspicions of me."

Cecily smiled impishly, grateful for the change of subject. "I think you've forgotten the reason for that," she reminded him. "Remember Doctor Whiting was here when you were first brought in."

Jack let out a shout of laughter. "So that was it!" he said. "I wondered why he seemed to think me such a queer fellow. He thinks me some cross between an actor and a coachman." Then, looking at her as if he sensed something was troubling her, he asked, "I wonder what your cousin would say to my true occupation?"

This mention of Alfred recalled Cecily's recent experience, and she could not smile. She turned away to hide her look of despair.

Jack laid a gentle hand on her shoulder. "What is it, Cecily? What have I said? Has Stourport been annoying you?"

Cecily shook her head, angry at herself for revealing her feelings. "It was nothing," she said with an attempt at lightness. She was determined not to bother him with this latest development, but her heart was feeling an unaccustomed oppression which the confinement of the past many weeks had only served to make worse.

She was determined not to give in to the dismals. Turning back to Jack, she suddenly proposed a change of plans. "Would you care to take a turn in Sir Waldo's carriage? I can handle the reins. Just yesterday you said you would like to see my skill."

Jack's look of concern disappeared and was replaced by admiration. He could not help but admire the lady's courage in the face of overwhelming discouragements.

"Yes, of course," he added, "with Sir Waldo's permission."

"Fiddle!" said Cecily. "My grandfather's permission goes without saying." She walked back towards the house with him, matching his slow pace, until they were met by Mr. Selby who was emerging from a door.

"Selby," she said, in a polite but firm tone, "have Bob harness Sir Waldo's team to his phaeton, if you please. Doctor Whiting has given his permission for Mr. Henley to go out, and I shall be taking him on a drive."

Mr. Selby looked at Jack with a shocked expression and spoke disapprovingly. "Sir Waldo's horses have not been out for some time, Miss Wolverton. I cannot think he would care to see you risk your safety."

Cecily raised her chin. "That is nonsense, Selby, and you know it. You know nothing about horses and you only wish to discourage me from going."

"But Sir Waldo..."

"You may tell Sir Waldo what you please. I am going out. We shall not venture much farther than the gate. Please have the goodness to do as I say."

Jack was leaning against the doorway, enjoying the spectacle of the six-foot Selby brought to heel by his diminutive mistress. Selby threw him a discreetly irreverent glance and gave in. As his back disappeared from view, Jack said to Cecily admiringly, "Well done! I am certain I would not have the courage to undertake a battle with Mr. Selby."

Cecily flushed and dimpled. "Of course you would," she protested. "Will you walk to the stable with me, or shall I collect you up here?"

Jack would not allow himself to be coddled to that extent, and insisted upon going with her.

When they were installed on the box, Bob having assisted Jack to climb up, Cecily took the reins and coaxed the horses out onto the drive. From there she took them at a brisk pace out the gate and onto the road leading to the village.

"Do not go into the village," Jack cautioned her.

She looked at him in surprise, asking, "Why not?"

Jack answered ruefully, "Sir Waldo may not mind your taking his carriage, but I doubt he would wish you to be seen in the village driving a common coachman."

She flushed. "Don't be silly. Of course he would not mind."

At first Jack said nothing, but when he saw she did not mean to turn the horses, he put one hand out to cover hers on the reins and said, "Turn them, please.

If you do not, I shall do it myself and will not ride out with you again."

Cecily looked up, startled by the mastery in his tone, and started to protest again. But when she saw the look in his eyes, she faltered and acceded to his wish. She slowed the horses to a walk and carefully turned them in a wide spot in the road. Then she brought them to a trot and took them past Sir Waldo's gate in the other direction.

Jack complimented her handling of them, adding as an afterthought some comments about the weather. It was a fine summer day. The birds were everywhere about and wild honeysuckle was growing alongside the road. But Jack's intention was not to draw Cecily's thoughts to the beauties of nature, but to redirect her rebellious energy. He knew something was bothering her, for he had never seen her in such a frame of mind.

But when she only answered him absently he realized something must have affected her strongly.

Coming right to the point, he said, "Perhaps now you will tell me what plagues you."

Surprised, she became alert and stopped the horses, saying, "As I said before, it is nothing. I have been quite confined, you know, and I thought a drive would help shake the cobwebs from my head."

"Come now," responded Jack. "You have been confined for more than two months without showing a sign of irritation. Perhaps you've been more subdued than when I first met you, but that is to be expected under these conditions. I know you well enough by now to tell when there is something amiss. What's Alfred done?"

She shook her head, saying briskly, "There's no need for you to concern yourself, Mr. Henley. I shall manage Alfred. Now, isn't that a pretty scene over there?" she asked, making a sweeping gesture with her hand to a wood beyond them.

"Cecily," he begged, taking light hold on her arm and speaking in a soft, coaxing voice. "Did you not say I might help you?"

She tried to withstand his gentle urging, but it was of little use. Something in his tone caused her to look up, and as her eyes met his, her resistance broke.

"I ought not to repeat it," she said, ashamed for her weakness. "But . . . Alfred has just offered for me."

Jack's brows snapped together. "He wants to marry you?" He released her arm suddenly and then asked, "What was your answer?" His eyes searched hers intently and he saw a rosy hue rise to her cheeks.

"I refused him, of course."

Jack released a slow breath of relief. But he was still angry. "Is there something you have not told me? *Did* he annoy you?"

Cecily hastened to deny it, but Jack's protective support seemed to have comforted her. "No, I assure you. His offer was made with propriety. But it was strange," she added truthfully. "He cannot love me, although he tried to suggest otherwise. Alfred has never shown the slightest affection for me. And when I refused he gave me to understand that he was offering for me to help rectify my unfortunate circumstances."

Jack frowned again, but his anger had vanished. "The man's a fool if that's the best reason he could give you." He ignored Cecily's sudden blush and went on, "But do you suppose he means it?"

Cecily shrugged her shoulders in a little gesture of helplessness. "I cannot say. If he does, it is a complete change of character. And why should he have waited so long if this had been his intention from the start?"

Jack mused for a moment. "I wish I knew," he said. "It seems there is more to this than we know. If only there were some way to find out just what his motives are. Did he accept your refusal? Will he be leaving?"

Cecily answered with some confusion. "I do not think so. He begged me to think about his proposal. I am afraid I allowed him to think I would do so, but you see, I was quite anxious to leave the room."

Jack smiled grimly. "Then he has more gumption than I gave him credit for. That is not to say I wish him success. But if I were he..."

He stopped, but she seemed compelled to meet his gaze. "Yes?" she asked almost in a whisper.

Despite all his efforts not to be carried away, at the look on her face Jack's heart swelled within him and he threw caution to the winds. He ran his finger lightly down her arm from the puff of her sleeve to the elbow and back again. He could almost feel the thrill that coursed through her. "I should never give up," he said. Then, unable to prevent himself from going on, he began hesitantly, "If I were a gentleman again... and not a 'servant of the road'..." He stopped speaking, his eyes scanning hers for a response.

Cecily could not hide the elation that rose up within her. She lowered her eyelids, but not before Jack saw the excitement in her expression. There was a moment's quiet. Then, as if she sensed the effort it was taking him not to say more, she took up the reins and began to turn the carriage.

"What will you do," she asked brightly, once this was done, "when your father takes you back into the fold?" There was only a slight quiver in her voice to betray her.

Jack laughed from pure exuberance. "When I am back in the fold? Let me see. I have been thinking about this. I shall first ask my father to give me a chance at managing his estate. He has always done it, you see, and I have had little to apply myself to. But I think after this experience, he will see that I really must have some occupation."

"I see," said Cecily. Her dimples deepened approvingly at this notion and she asked, "Do you think you shall like being a gentleman again?"

Jack chuckled and blurted out, "One eats a damned sight better! Do you remark the difference between the first meal you gave me and the one we had last night?"

Cecily pouted playfully. "If you mean to complain about your porridge, sir, you shall grossly offend me. I assure you, that had I been certain of your parentage, you would still have been given the same."

They carried on like this until Cecily, remembering that Jack had only just begun using his injured leg, turned the horses back into the gate. Jack protested. In truth, he had not noticed any fatigue. The sudden elevation of his spirits had given him a burst of energy and he was eager to resume his activities. The sooner he returned now to his work, the sooner would he achieve his newly found goals.

That afternoon, he and Cecily met again in Sir Waldo's room to entertain that gentleman before dinner. There was a gaiety in their laughter that spurred the old man on, and he told his more outrageous stories. A time or two, Jack caught Cecily blushing. But he did not know that it was the warmth of his smile upon her, rather than her grandfather's words, that had brought the colour to her cheeks.

ALFRED DID NOT LEAVE the manor. For the next week he remained as a nuisance to them all. Cecily tried not to mind him, but it was a constant strain trying to avoid being alone with him, and his surliness to Jack increased as he perceived his cousin's preference. Mealtimes, above all, were tarnished with the unpleasantness of his tongue, for he grew more and more overt in his dislike for his fellow guest. It was all Cecily could do to prevent a challenge from being exchanged. But Alfred, not really intent upon an exchange of blows with a more athletic specimen, was always careful to give a double meaning to his most offensive remarks.

Cecily could only marvel at it. Why did he remain when it was patently obvious she would not accept his offer? He had tried several times to speak to her alone, but Jack was always nearby. He had made himself her shield, and Alfred was repeatedly foiled in his attempts to find her unguarded. When Jack was otherwise occupied, Cecily could easily seek the shelter of her grandfather's room. And no one could say that her behaviour was inappropriate, for she and Jack behaved with total propriety. They met in the public rooms, and only the glow in his eyes and the rose in her cheeks betrayed the thoughts that were shared between them.

The only times they ventured to appear alone together were on their daily walks about the garden. These walks had the sanction of both Doctor Whiting and Sir Waldo, for they were ostensibly made to restore Jack to his proper condition. Alfred might have joined them if he liked, but he had never done so. And certainly, Jack thought, a man in love would have insisted upon it.

Jack had not spoken of his own feelings. There were times during those lingering walks when he had been tempted to do so—when the smell of a rose as they passed, mixed with the feel of Cecily's hair brushing close to his shoulder, confused his senses. What had started as a flirtation had become much more. Jack felt that he and Cecily had been drawn together by their similar circumstances, which had formed a fast bond between them. At times, when the temptation to speak was at its greatest, he would have to brace himself and recall the months ahead of him before he could make her his offer. He hoped they were only months, and not years, but he could not be certain, and until he was he did not have the right to speak. He knew, however, that his eyes had spoken for him, and that hers had given their answer.

At the end of the sixth week of his convalescence, Jack knew it was time to make ready for his return to the mail. He had not corresponded with the proprietor of the coach since the accident. Davies would have made his report and notified Mr. Waddell at the Castle Hotel in Birmingham. It would be up to Jack to apply for his old position back. Accordingly, he formed his intention to ask Sir Waldo for the use of his carriage the following day, in order to drive into Hockley Heath to meet the mail.

CHAPTER ELEVEN

JACK HAD MENTIONED NOTHING of his decision to Cecily, not wishing to hasten his leave of her. The next morning he breakfasted early as usual with both Cecily and Alfred. Alfred had given up his practice of sleeping late of mornings, and when Cecily had commented on it, he had merely observed dryly that the early hour at which one retires in the country must have been the cause of it. But the early hours and the resulting rest had done nothing to restore Alfred's pasty complexion. If anything, his pallor had worsened, and both Cecily and Jack misliked his nervous manner. There was a hint of desperation in his eyes, a tendency to jump at the slightest noise, both of which only seemed to increase each day of his stay.

He was toying with his breakfast, ignoring the conversation going on around him, when the footman brought him a message on a salver.

"This was delivered to the house by hand this morning, your lordship," said the servant with a bow. "It was brought up by one of the men from the Rose and Crown."

Cecily and Jack watched while Alfred took the note and held it up to inspect it through his quizzing glass.

At the sight of the writing upon it, however, he blanched and seemed almost to shudder.

"What is it, Alfred?" asked Cecily. "A message from Stourport? Is there something wrong?" She could not conceal a note of concern in her voice.

Alfred tittered nervously, but his smile held a touch of menace. "Of course not, my dear Cecily. How your mind does turn to Stourport! It would be most touching, were it not for your refusal to do a simple thing which could put your mind at rest about it forever. I wonder you do not recognize it."

Cecily ignored the clear reference to his proposal and said, "But the note, Alfred. Is there anything in it to necessitate your leaving us?" She hoped her voice did not sound too hopeful.

"Your concern is most affecting," answered Alfred with a stiff inclination of the head. "But the matter is much too trivial to annoy you with."

He seemed, as he made these remarks, to be exercising a great deal of self-control, so Cecily did not press him. Instead, she continued her conversation with Jack, only occasionally addressing a comment to her cousin. When she did, she invariably found that he was not attending. Nor was he making headway with his meal. He seemed preoccupied, distant, and yet he fidgeted continuously with his fork and napkin. Once, when she had addressed him and received no response, Cecily threw Jack a puzzled look. He answered her with a slight shrug and a raised eyebrow.

Immediately after this, Jack rose from the table and begged her to excuse him.

"I have asked to have a word with your grandfather," he said. "I would like his permission to take a carriage down into the village to meet the mail coach."

Cecily's eyes opened wide with distress and then fell quickly. "Of course," she said, rather breathlessly. "You must. But there will be no trouble, I am certain. Grandpapa will gladly lend you one of his carriages." She stood and prepared to accompany him.

"To the village, you say? Are you going to the village?" asked Alfred suddenly in a high-pitched squeak. They turned to look at him, both startled by his inexplicable interest.

"That's right," said Jack, frowning. "Is there some commission I might carry out for you?"

Alfred closed his eyes and shook his head convulsively. "No. Thank you," he answered. "Cecily, I beg you will excuse me. I find I am not well. I intend to spend the day in bed, and I do not wish to be disturbed."

"A very good idea," said Cecily. "I do not like to mention it again, Alfred, but in truth, you have not looked well since the day you arrived. I have wondered, in fact, why you would choose to go visiting when you are obviously not yourself."

"As to that, my dear Cecily, you may ask your own conscience whether it is not in your power to make me feel better," answered Alfred waspishly. He placed the back of one hand to his forehead. "But for the moment, I am not well enough to discuss it. I shall take my leave of you until this evening."

Clutching his message, he made his way from the room, but appeared so feeble that Cecily had to restrain herself from offering her arm. When she turned to Jack, she found he was barely concealing a smile.

"Do you suppose he is trying to win you through sympathy?" he asked when Alfred was out of range. He clearly thought her cousin's behaviour a pose.

Cecily could not help smiling, but she shook her head all the same. "I do not think so. What I said to him was true. He has not looked well since he arrived. And *that* was before I refused him. It is one of the reasons I did not turn him away at the door."

Jack shrugged again. "Well," he said, "it's a mystery. But I must be off if I am to intercept the mail."

Cecily felt a little catch in her throat. She endeavoured to make her voice sound cheerful. "Yes. You must hurry."

She accompanied Jack to Sir Waldo's room and left them together. Then she sought the solitude of her own chamber.

Sir Waldo frowned as he listened to Jack's request. He did not give his answer immediately. "When do you suppose your father will be through with this nonsense of his?" he asked instead.

Jack stiffened. "When he wishes to be," he replied. His own feelings about his father's methods had undergone such a material change, that he was now of the opinion that the cure prescribed for his profligacy was the most brilliant ever devised. He did not feel Sir Waldo could claim any reason to challenge his father's judgement.

But Jack's stiff reaction had not gone undetected. Sir Waldo snorted once or twice to show his displeasure, but he refrained from commenting further. He gave Jack his permission to use one of his carriages, adjuring him to take care not to overturn it or his leg would be permanently lost. Jack grinned at this unnecessary advice, and was about to leave the room when Sir Waldo called him back.

"When shall you leave us, my boy?" the old man asked in a subdued voice.

"In another week, sir," said Jack gently, stepping to the side of the bed.

Sir Waldo nodded listlessly. "Not before that jackanapes of a lordship is gone, I hope."

Jack frowned deeply. "Not if I can help it, sir. He seems strangely unwilling to move. In fact, he has taken to his bed."

Sir Waldo's ears perked up. "Is that the truth? Sick, is he? Well, I'm glad to hear it. Maybe we can bury him before he causes any more trouble."

Jack suppressed a smile. As long as Sir Waldo remained capable of his scurrilous attacks on Alfred, he ought to be all right. "At least, he does not seem to be in any condition to annoy you," he responded.

Sir Waldo gripped his hand. "It isn't me, Jack," he said, turning a worried countenance up to view. "It's Cecy I'm worried about. That blackguard's robbed her of everything that's hers. I've got two thousand pounds I can give her, but that's all. The rest goes on to my sister Mary's boy. A good boy, for all that, but he's not like Cecy."

Jack clasped the old man's hand tightly. He wanted to tell Sir Waldo of his feelings and reassure him that Cecily's future would be secure, but caution told him it was still too early. He had not yet won his father's approval.

"I wish I could say more," he finally allowed, "but I hope you know that I will come any time you think Miss Wolverton needs assistance. I count on you to send for me."

Sir Waldo lay back and released his hand. "Good lad," he said with a sigh. "Though it's not so much *now* that worries me. It's after I'm gone. For *she* will not call on you, you know. She's too independent." He must have sensed the distress he was causing Jack, for he turned to him with a weary grin. "Let us only hope Alfred beats me to the undertaker, shall we?"

"That's the spirit, sir." Jack returned Sir Waldo's smile and bade him goodbye.

He left the room, however, not in the highest spirits. Sir Waldo's ill health was a matter of concern to him, for where would Cecily find herself without her grandfather? Jack knew by now that he was head over heels in love with her. And despite his repeated warnings to himself, he had allowed himself to make his feelings known to her. Silently, to be sure, but nonetheless evidently, and he was tolerably certain that those feelings were returned. Cecily's manner to him had undergone a gradual change from coolness to caution, progressing rapidly to trust. Now her glowing smiles upon seeing him were almost too much for his powers of resistance. If once more he allowed himself to touch her, he would be undone. He could only hope that his own fortune would be restored before Sir Waldo gave up his struggles. He knew he could not ask Cecily to share his life as it was.

AN HOUR LATER, Jack pulled up Sir Waldo's horses before the Rose and Crown. He took a moment to catch his breath before descending from the carriage. The effort to manage the drive without giving his leg too great a jolt had taken more strength than he was now accustomed to using. He had had to hurry too, for the conversation with Sir Waldo had lasted longer than he had anticipated. But he found, upon entering the inn, that he had arrived in time, for the mail was expected any minute.

A bustle of noise and excitement heralded its approach. The ostlers ran about taking up handfuls of harness and prepared to freshen the horses, and Mr. Rose drew two pints at the tap to send out to the men. Jack stood from the chair where he had been waiting and asked for the privilege of carrying them outside. This drew a grin from the good-natured innkeeper, who grandly presented him with the two frothy mugs.

Jack limped out into the yard just as the horses came to a halt. He watched as the driver stepped down from the box and then offered him his mug. The man accepted it with a condescending air before turning to extract the parcels from the foreboot. He seemed a cheerful fellow, full of his own importance and certain of meriting admiration.

The back of the coach was what interested Jack the most, however, for there he spied his old guard, Davies. At first, Davies did not see him, for he was occupied with the important task of recording his time in the logbook. The mail sack for Hockley Heath had been taken from the cache beneath his feet and was hanging from his shoulder. When he glanced up, however, to see whose face belonged to the boots before him, he started and let a rare grin escape.

"Eh, young fella," he said. "I didn't know t'was you. Up and goin' on your feet already now, are you?"

Jack assured him he was and presented him with the pint. The guard waved him away with a chuckle until he could deliver his precious sack, but promised to return shortly. Jack took the time to look over the harness that the ostlers were rehitching and to admire its neat appearance. Mr. Rose was a coach owner on this ground and took good care of his property.

Davies returned quickly and Jack begged his attention. The coach made only a five-minute stop, so they would have little time to chat.

"How was your report received on the accident?" Jack asked him.

Davies shook his head sadly at first, but then grinned impishly at Jack's show of consternation. "Nay, lad. You've nought to worry about. It was the proprietor's fault in Shipston. The coach ought to 'ave been looked over better that mornin'. It was a weak spot up under the carriage—you just missed it, that's all."

"They don't think I ought to have seen it?"

Davies shook his head. "Perhaps you ought, but they're not blamin' you for it. It was too hard to detect." He looked Jack over and lifted an enquiring eyebrow. "Aren't they treatin' you well up at the manor? Are you ready to come back into service?"

Jack took a deep breath. "I'll be ready in a week. Do you think they'll give me my old ground back?"

Davies shrugged, but his expression was encouraging. "I'll put in a good word for you. And who knows but what the passengers might not insist upon it." He cocked his head towards the front of the coach. "This fella's not as sober as you got to be."

Jack laughed and thanked him. Davies clapped him on the back and prepared to climb back onto his perch. But before the mail coach could take off with a lurch, Jack took a few steps back and away from it and almost collided with a gentleman who was strolling into the inn.

"Watch your step, my good man," said the other man testily. "You nearly trod on my good boots and disturbed the polish. You ought to watch where you are going."

Jack apologized good-naturedly and turned to smile up at Davies. He found, however, that his friend was not smiling so broadly.

"Popinjay," muttered the guard under his breath. "That fella' rode up from London with us yesterday," he explained. "A conceited peacock if I've ever seen one. Talked the whole way about his friendship with Lord Stourport, lorded it over the rest of the passengers, and forgot to leave his shillin's to boot. If you want my opinion, that one's no better than he should be, and if you want to step on him, Jack, you've got my blessin'."

As Davies put the horn to his lips to sound the departure of the mail, Jack turned quickly to look after the subject of their conversation, who had just disappeared inside the inn. Jack waved goodbye to the guard with a thoughtful expression, and then turned to follow the self-proclaimed friend of Lord Stourport into the public room.

CHAPTER TWELVE

As Jack entered the smoke-filled room, he was greeted by a gentle hum of voices. It was approaching midday, and people had begun to drift into the inn for a spot of ale before heading home for their dinner. As soon as Jack's eyes became accustomed to the dim light, he espied the gentleman Davies had indicated, sitting at a table.

Mr. Rose was busy at the tap, so Jack limped over and sat as close to him as possible. After a few minutes, the innkeeper asked him for his order.

"Saw you talking to the guard on the mail this morning," ventured Mr. Rose. "Happen you'll be taking up the reins again soon." He regarded Jack with interest.

"That's right," said Jack. "It's time for me to get back into harness."

They chatted on about the mail business for awhile, until Jack, who had never taken his eyes off his quarry, asked Mr. Rose about him.

The innkeeper quirked an eyebrow in the direction of his guest and snorted with disgust. "That fella'? I don't know what you would want with him. Name of Sudbury, or some such thing. Tries to pass himself off as a gentleman. Even asked me for one of my private parlours, but I knew better than to waste one on him! More of a gentleman's *gentleman*, I would say, and I've entertained enough of the gentry to know the difference. Claims he's a friend of that Lord Stourport what's staying up at the manor with Sir Waldo. But what I say is, if he is such a friend of his, what's he doing down here instead of calling up at the manor?"

"What indeed?" agreed Jack, staring at the man with interest. The name Sudbury had made his ears prick up, and a wave of excitement rolled through him as he realized he was on to something.

"Is he staying on tick?" he asked Mr. Rose suddenly.

The innkeeper shook his head. "Not he. I wouldn't venture to give him a bed unless I knew he could come up with the reckoning. There's something too havey-cavey about him if you ask me. But I will say this," he admitted, "he's had no trouble paying his way at the bar. Waves his purse all around so that everyone can see how full it is. And he ordered himself a big meal last night and gave our serving girl quite a tip for it. Course, it was easy to see what he had in mind, but our Betsy's not that sort of a girl, if you get my meaning."

"I see," mused Jack. And indeed, his thoughts were rapidly forming a connection that could explain the man's identity. He was certain that this Sudbury was the same fellow who had so lately been in the employ of Alfred—his former valet, in fact. If the name had been needed to identify him positively, his style and bearing alone would have betrayed his calling, despite the clothes of a gentleman. No one except a personal manservant would carry himself so stiffly, and his perfect, white neckcloth, the absence of any wrinkles in his coat, and the impossible shine on his boots proclaimed the hand of an expert. Evidently Sudbury, in spite of coming into recent wealth, performed his own toilet. Jack doubted he would be satisfied with anything less.

But how had he come into money? It was true that this might be possible for any valet. Wasn't it said that Beau Brummell himself had a valet for a grandfather? But changes in circumstances did not, as a rule, come about so drastically. And not usually without the patronage of an employer. Jack knew that Alfred had broken with his former valet, and he now suspected that the reason for the rupture had been more extreme than Alfred had led them to believe.

After thanking Mr. Rose for the ale and the conversation, Jack took his glass and walked over to Sudbury in a modified stagger. He took pains to appear as if Mr. Rose's pint of ale had not been his first.

He was passing Sudbury's table, pretending not to notice him, when he suddenly stopped and stared. "'Hoy there, friend!" he cried, lowering his face to gaze myopically at the valet. "Aren't you the fellow I nearly stepped on outside here?"

Sudbury drew his head back as far as he could, but Jack responded by bringing his face closer. The accosted valet spoke haughtily. "I am, indeed, my good man, but that does not qualify you as an acquaintance. Move along now and do not bother me."

Jack laughed and, as if he had not heard Sudbury, took a chair across the table. "Well now," he said. "I can't have you goin' away all offended now, can I? What'll it be? What will you have?"

Sudbury's nostrils flared with offence and he drew himself up with a rigid back. "I have no intention of drinking with you, you lout. I ought not to have come into the public rooms at all, and I would not have if there had been any private ones available. But I will not be insulted by any clodpole who fancies a talk with his betters."

He might have spared his words, for Jack, feigning a drunken fog, seemed not to have heard them. Jack called loudly to the innkeeper and ordered two pints of his best bitter. He had deliberately placed himself so that Sudbury could not rise, unless Jack moved the table backwards.

Mr. Rose brought their drinks instantly and threw Jack a puzzled look as he set them down. Sudbury was protesting at that moment that if his dear friend, Lord Stourport, were only there, he would be certain to be drinking with him privately without such rude intrusions.

Mr. Rose, perceiving a sly wink from Jack, ventured to remark, "If it's Lord Stourport you'll be wanting, Jack here can tell you all about him. He's been staying up at the manor these five weeks and more." He smiled at the look of incredulity which came over Sudbury's face.

"You?" emitted the valet in shocked tones. "*You* have been staying up at the manor?" He examined Jack's clothing with repugnance.

"I have," confirmed Jack, pretending not to notice the offending note. "Not as a guest, o' course, but in the house, mind you. I broke my leg when the mail come through more than a month ago. Sir Waldo, he's been puttin' me up. But I'm up and around now," he added cheerfully. "Won't be much longer before I'm back to work."

As he had hoped, Sudbury quickly brought him back to the subject. "But you have seen Lord Stourport?" he enquired eagerly. "You must have heard me mention how great a friend he is. Why there is no one nearer to Lord Stourport than I!" This last assertion seemed to amuse him greatly and he ended by chuckling to himself.

"Well, now!" said Jack in the heartiest tones. "Isn't that a rare thing? Why you ought to come back up with me to the manor! I could drive you in Sir Waldo's carriage."

Sudbury started to speak and then hesitated, one finger to his lips. "Thank you, my good man," he said finally. "But I do not think that will serve. Sir Waldo is not expecting me, you see. I do not think that would be the proper way to go about it." He seemed to be speaking this last almost to himself.

Jack shrugged. "As you like," he said. "But I'm sure Lord Stourport would be happy to see you. He's not been too well, they say. Stayed in his bed this morning." He watched his companion closely for a reaction.

The news seemed to please Sudbury inordinately. "Not well, you say?" he said, smiling. "That is too bad. I hope he will not regret coming to see Sir Waldo. I advised him against it."

"Oh?" said Jack, scarcely able to control his interest. When that remark drew nothing, however, he raised his eyebrows significantly. "They do say," he said in a low voice, "that he's come to offer for Miss Cecily, Sir Waldo's granddaughter. She's his cousin, you know."

Sudbury's eyes contracted and he stiffened. Then he looked at Jack disdainfully. "If you mean Miss Wolverton, young man, I am well acquainted with the matter," he said sharply. But Jack could see he was not pleased. "I warned him against it," the valet mumbled.

Jack pretended not to have heard this comment, which was clearly not intended for him. "Well, 'tis of no moment to me, but you really ought to come up to the manor. His lordship's not lookin' too perky."

Sudbury came back to attention with a start. "Has he hired a new valet?"

Jack could hardly restrain a smile. He shrugged. "Not that I knows of," he said without interest. "I never had too many doings with valets and the like, to own the truth. Too high in the instep, if you ask me. Not a good fella like you." He leered at Sudbury with an overly friendly smile. It was a temptation he could not resist.

Sudbury responded with a look of disgust and was about to leave the table, when Jack ventured one last word. "Happen his lordship don't even know you're here," he said casually.

The former valet could not resist refuting the sly implication. "There, my good man, you are mistaken," he asserted. "I have sent my card up to his lordship, and he has every intention of calling on me at his earliest convenience."

Jack gaped in silent awe at the impression these words were intended to create, and Sudbury bowed condescendingly and wished him good day. If he had not been upon such serious business with the valet, Jack would then have had a good laugh. But he could not stay amused. Too many thoughts were crowding into his brain.

He strove to put them together. Sudbury had admitted to sending his card up to Alfred. That would have to have been the note at breakfast that morning, for Davies had said that Sudbury came in by yesterday's mail. And the note had clearly upset Alfred. He had been even further distressed to learn that Jack intended to go down to the village that day. No doubt he feared a chance meeting of exactly the sort that had occurred. Knowing Sudbury as he did, he must certainly have known that he would puff their acquaintance to the limit. The two men were well aligned in their respective conceit.

Jack had his own suspicions of the relationship that now existed between these two men, but he decided not to waste any more time thinking it through at the inn. Cecily should be told of Sudbury's arrival as soon as possible, he reflected seriously. He had a notion that whatever was going on between the two men had more to do with her than with anyone else.

Jack hastened back to the manor. He had to wait impatiently to speak to her, for Cecily had retreated to Sir Waldo's room during his absence. But before too long he was able to join her for a small midday repast in the dining room. Then, of course, Alfred was with them. In spite of his morning malady and his intention to stay abed all day, it seemed he could not resist satisfying his curiosity about whether Jack had run into his former valet. He posed Jack several innocuous questions in an apparent endeavour to discover the information. But Jack's innocent look deceived him and he retired to his bed that afternoon not a whit the wiser. He did try once again to persuade Cecily to grant him a private audience, but she reminded him firmly that Jack's walk must come first. That the doctor insisted upon it was her excuse. Alfred's spirits were so under siege, however, that he gave up the struggle with no more than one hateful look at Jack before stumbling, with the assistance of a footman, up to bed.

Jack waited until they had reached the far end of the garden walk before he told Cecily his news. There, seated under the shade of a trellis of rose leaves he related his discovery of the morning.

"Sudbury!" cried Cecily upon hearing his name. "Whatever could he mean by coming here in such a guise? Do you suppose his intention is to embarrass

Alfred? Was he so offended when Alfred turned him off that he chose this manner of avenging himself?"

Jack regarded her intently as he spoke. "I suspect there is a good deal more to it than that, Cecily. Mr. Rose informed me that Sudbury has money, enough of it to demand all the comforts of a gentleman, even though his manner is somewhat less than convincing."

"But where would he get . . . ?" Cecily began. Then she stopped as a thought struck her. She raised eager eyes to Jack and said, "From Alfred! Do you think he could have taken money from Alfred?"

Jack nodded, glad that she had quickly come to the same conclusion. "I am convinced of it. Sudbury told me he had sent his card up to the manor to notify your cousin of his being here. If that was the note Alfred received at breakfast this morning, we have plenty of evidence as to its effect upon him. He has scarcely been able to stand. I can only conclude that Sudbury pursued Alfred here to extort more money from him."

"But that would be blackmail!" Cecily cried.

Jack raised his brows expressively, but said nothing. He still wanted to see what interpretation she would put upon the evidence.

When he did not speak, Cecily frowned and added, "Then that would mean Alfred has something quite serious to hide."

Jack bent closer to her and took her hands in his. "Cecily, I must tell you that when I talked to Sudbury, he twice indicated that he had warned Alfred not to come here. Oh, it was not expressed so clearly," he added quickly when he saw her alarm, "but he did not think I was attending properly. I made it appear that I was a trifle foxed."

He was glad to see that his explanation had relieved her. Cecily pursed her lips to suppress a smile at his antics.

He continued, watching anxiously for her reaction. "Cecily, do you think as I do? Can you think of something Sudbury might know about, which Alfred would wish to remain concealed?"

She gazed at him solemnly. The answer was already on her lips. "The theft of my father's will."

Jack nodded grimly. Unconsciously, he began to caress the small hands he still held. "My thoughts precisely. If, as you say, Alfred did not go into your father's study during his visit to your father's deathbed, then he must have instructed Sudbury to do so and nick the will. In that case, Sudbury would know quite enough about the proceeding to cause Alfred much damage, were he to divulge it."

It was Cecily's turn to nod. Her cheeks seemed flushed with suppressed excitement. All at once Jack realized what he had been doing with her hands and, after clearing his throat of its sudden constriction, released them. They smiled at one another self-consciously. He would have liked nothing better than to take her in his arms at that moment, but restrained himself with the reminder that they must carry this talk to its conclusion.

Cecily's next sentence was delivered in a voice which sounded robbed of breath. "But surely Sudbury could not reveal the existence of the will without endangering himself as well! Alfred ought to know that."

Her words made Jack frown with renewed concentration. "That is so. And if Alfred has the will, what good would it do Sudbury to accuse him of anything? Alfred could simply claim that they were the vengeful ravings of a dismissed servant. Sudbury could not prove his assertions without severely endangering himself, as you say."

They both were silent as they pondered this puzzle. Then Cecily said in a sobered voice, "Well, at least I know now why Alfred offered for me."

Jack looked at her questioningly.

She explained, "He wants to assure himself that, even if the existence of the will is revealed somehow, he shall still have control of the estate. If the property were found to be mine after all, as my husband he would be the rightful owner. It would be unlikely I would do anything to send my own husband to prison."

Jack felt a spurt of anger rise within him at these words, but he had to agree with her assessment. "The fellow's even more of a snake than I thought," he said shortly. He stood and began to pace up and down to relieve some of his tension. His leg was by now feeling much stronger. "I wish there were some way of finding exactly what hold Sudbury has over Alfred. Then we might see a way of extracting the truth from your cousin."

Cecily watched him walk back and forth in front of her. She was smiling a little self-consciously, as if still disturbed by the touch of his hand. "Do you think," she ventured, "that Alfred's reason has been damaged by his sense of guilt? He is almost prostrate. Could he not be suffering from an overwrought conscience? Sudbury could have been preying upon it for some time now."

Jack shook his head, unconvinced. "Not your cousin Alfred," he said dryly. "I see no Lady Macbeth in him. His pursuit of you does not suggest to me the workings of contrition."

"No," she agreed with a sigh. "Then I do not see that we have advanced much in our knowledge."

Jack resumed his seat beside her and faced her, saying earnestly, "Do not give up hope yet, Cecily. I am certain that Sudbury intends to meet Alfred—perhaps this very night. We may discover some knowledge of your father's will before many days have passed. I can almost promise it."

Cecily gazed at him speechlessly for a moment. Then she covered her face with her hands. "Oh, Jack!" she said, with a great sigh of relief. "Do you know what you have done? Can you even imagine? It is not so much the possibility that I may recover my property, although it would be wonderful to return to my home, and I should be glad of the money. It is the knowledge, the actual certainty, that my father did indeed mean to provide for me." She looked up at him, glowing with happiness, though her eyes were filled with tears. "And to think that if you had not gone into the village this morning, we might never have known this."

Now Jack was ready to take her into his arms. Her eyes invited him. His heart beat strongly with the desire to cover her pretty lips with kisses. He took her by the shoulders and she raised her face shyly to meet him. But suddenly, something she had just said arrested him. His brows came together, and his hands dropped to his sides.

If all went as he expected, Cecily would have her fortune restored to her. Could he let it be said that she had kissed a coachman on the Royal Mail? Was he not still known in the village as Jack, the coachman? Jack would not allow a hint of scandal to touch the woman he loved.

He became aware that Cecily was watching him with a hurt and puzzled expression. He stood and walked a few paces away from her to regain his composure.

"It makes me very happy to know that I have restored some measure of peace to you," he said in a constricted voice.

Cecily had risen also and taken a step towards him. "Jack, is anything amiss?"

Jack shook his head as if doing so would rid him of his feelings, and then turned to face her, smiling.

"No, of course not," he said. "How could there be? I was just thinking that there is every chance you will be a great heiress once again."

She stared at him, still wondering, until comprehension dawned. "Yes, I shall be," she admitted. "And all because of you."

Jack shook his head again in denial. "That is of no consequence."

"It is to me," she said in a quiet voice. When he did not speak, she added, "And it will make no difference that I can see except that I shall be more secure. I have no intention of changing."

Jack smiled sadly at her. "I am certain you will not, not in essentials, at least. But you will soon be caught up in a different world. You will not isolate yourself here in the country. Society will not let you."

Now having a clear understanding of Jack's distress, Cecily felt confident that she could dispel his concerns. She smiled warmly and spoke evenly so as to reassure him. "We shall see about that. If I choose to stay here visiting my grandfather until—" she blushed and lowered her eyes "—until it suits me to leave, who is to say I cannot?"

He could not mistake her meaning. She was telling him of her intention to wait for him. But he could not let her make such a sacrifice. Sir Geoffrey might decide to keep him in his present state for years. He might decide that Jack was not worthy of his regard. In that case, only his father's death would restore Jack to his position. Could he ask Cecily to wait for that? Should her name be coupled with someone who had been a common labourer for years? Her stature would surely suffer. And Jack knew that she had suffered so much from one scandal that she must not be exposed to another.

"You must not do that," he told her earnestly. "You might discover..." He struggled to find the right words. "You might discover that you had wasted your youth. You ought to be living the way you were intended to live. If you were to wait—" He broke off suddenly before he could imply more than he ought.

She looked at him sombrely. Her next words dropped into the painful silence like pebbles into a well. "I see no need to wait at all."

"Don't say that," he said sharply, feeling remorseful as Cecily hung her head in shame. She had offered to take him as he was, without the redemption of his father's blessing. But as much as he wanted her, he could not allow her to make such an uneven bargain.

"You must go into Society. You will surely marry." The words issued from his lips mechanically. He saw her shoulders stiffen slightly as if from a blow.

After a moment's silence, she said in a small voice, "Has no one ever told you, Jack, that pride is a sin? You are rather more like your father than you realize."

The sound of hurt in her voice was almost enough to make Jack relent, but he steeled himself. Now he became conscious that he had been squeezing his hands tightly into fists, and his leg was aching again from the strain of standing so stiffly.

"We ought to go at once to your grandfather and tell him what we suspect," he said wearily.

She looked up and then her eyes fell. "Yes, you are right."

Jack hesitated a moment before offering her his arm. She took it slowly, still refusing to look up at him. He laid his other hand on hers and gripped it tightly. Only then did she appease him with a sad smile. He hoped she knew that if he had wounded her, it was not half so deeply as he had hurt himself.

CHAPTER THIRTEEN

THE FAMILIAR JOURNEY to Sir Waldo's rooms was made in silence and mutual sadness. When they had greeted Sir Waldo and recounted their tale, it was obvious they could not have brought better news, for Sir Waldo was delighted.

"Sudbury, come to blackmail the weasely Alfred!" he exclaimed. "If that don't beat all! How I would love to see the scoundrel's face at this moment, knowing the torture he must be going through! Ah, it would give me another fifty years, at least!" He leaned back on his cushions and uttered a long sigh.

Jack and Cecily had to smile at Sir Waldo's perverse humour, despite the ache that surrounded them. They had both taken pains not to let him notice their misery, but if he had been more perceptive at the time he might have seen it. The news they had to give him was enough to make him oblivious to undercurrents.

"What do we do now?" he asked eagerly. "I'm a magistrate, you know. I could have them both up before me and wring the truth out of them."

Jack put up one hand to suggest caution. "Not yet, Sir Waldo. The time will come for that when we are certain of our evidence. If we confront them now, they can simply deny any knowledge of the will, and no one can dispute them. I think it best we wait until we can prove their culpability."

Sir Waldo smiled grimly, but the spark in his eyes showed he appreciated Jack's suggestion. "Then what do you mean to do?"

"Follow Lord Stourport," Jack answered. He could feel Cecily's eyes upon him but he refused to meet them. "I have it from Sudbury himself that he expects a visit from Lord Stourport. The gentleman can hardly refuse. Sooner or later his lordship will have to confront Sudbury, and when he does, I shall be there."

"But, Jack!" protested Cecily. "Your leg..."

"...is fine as fivepence," he said, finishing her sentence. Nevertheless, he sought to reassure her. "If I am well enough to go back to driving the mail, I ought to be up to any rig. Alfred should give me no trouble at all. In his condition it should be easy enough to follow him."

Sir Waldo snorted. "Never did move faster than a snail's pace. You needn't worry about Jack, Cecy," he told his granddaughter. "There's nothing that namby-pamby Alfred could do to Jack, here. Why he's twice the size and twice the man. But what do you suppose the meeting to be about?" he asked Jack.

Jack shrugged. "I shall only know when the meeting takes place and I do not think it will be long in coming. Because, if we are right, and Sudbury has information that can damage Alfred, he cannot afford to keep the man waiting. He'll be much too worried that Sudbury will do something precipitous. Sudbury hinted that he might do just that to me himself. He almost accepted my offer to drive him up here in the carriage."

The old man laughed. "You offered, did you? I would have liked to have seen Alfred's face when his former valet came driving up to the manor with one of our guests. That would have sent him reeling, I'll warrant."

"I confess, I had some such object in mind, sir," said Jack, grinning appreciatively. "But whatever Sudbury's game is, it's obviously much too important to him to waste on a foolish prank. He's waiting for something bigger. I just wish I knew exactly what he is threatening. But never mind. With a little luck, we'll soon know."

Sir Waldo regarded him seriously from under his grizzled eyebrows. "If you manage to find what happened to Stephen's will, my boy, I will be forever in your debt. I would have gone after Alfred with a whip and made him tell us if I hadn't been confined to this godforsaken bed. But seeing as I was, there never was much to do about it."

Jack was moved by the feelings of helplessness he knew were behind Sir Waldo's words. "Of course not," he said. "And it was only by the purest luck that I stumbled upon this news myself. Much as you would have liked to go after Alfred with that whip," he jested, "if he had not confessed, you would have been in the soup."

Sir Waldo's good humour returned. "I'll wager I could have got it out of that little weasel, though," he said, raising his eyebrows significantly.

Jack laughed. "No doubt you are right there, sir. There's nothing of the stoic about our Alfred, is there?"

Sir Waldo chuckled, and then insisted upon being told more of Jack's plans. There was not much left to say, however, and soon Jack retired from the room. He fervently hoped that Alfred would make a move that evening, for Jack could not afford to stay in the house much longer under any circumstances. The conversation with Cecily that afternoon had convinced him that he had been playing a dangerous game: first, in carrying on a flirtation with her, and later, in fooling himself that he would soon be able to claim her. As long as their circumstances had been similarly altered, he had been able to justify his pursuit of her. But now... The outcome of Sudbury's confrontation with Alfred would surely affect more than just Cecily's fortune.

JACK DID NOT have long to wait. Alfred came down to dinner that evening, but did not linger over his port. He claimed a headache as the reason for his recent indisposition, but Jack noticed he was feigning the yawns he covered with his hand as he bid them good night.

"I trust you do not intend to sit up together, Cousin," Alfred said pointedly to Cecily. "I do think, do you not, that it would appear most particular, especially to the servants."

This time, Cecily did flush at his words. She had not directed one look at Jack throughout the evening, although she had carried on the conversation as though nothing were amiss. Only Jack was aware of the difference in her manner towards him. She glanced at him now, though, as if she could feel his eyes upon her. "That is nonsense, Alfred," she said coolly. "But, of course I do not intend to sit up with Mr. Henley. I shall accompany you upstairs and attend to my grandfather. Good night, Mr. Henley," she said with grave formality.

"Good night, Miss Wolverton."

Jack followed a few paces behind as the others made their way up the stairs. He wanted Alfred to have the impression that he had decided to turn in for the night, as well. Once in his room, he discarded his neckcloth and called the footman to remove his brogues. Then, after dismissing the servant, he waited until the house seemed quieted down for the night, before tiptoeing in his stockinged feet back down the stairway and out the side entrance. He had already chosen a handy place of concealment on a knoll, behind a privet hedge, where he would be able to see if anyone approached the house or left it.

He had covered his white shirt with a darker cape and carried his shoes along with him. It was a lengthy and tedious wait out in the garden in the cold night air, but not long after two o'clock, his efforts were rewarded. A slight squeak from the direction of the house alerted him to the fact that someone had opened a door. And before long, he was able to make out the silhouette of a man moving hesitantly across the lawn.

It was Alfred, he had no doubt, and not making in the direction of the stables.

Keeping as low to the ground as possible, Jack followed him, the only difficulty being the stiffness of his leg. But he soon saw the unlikelihood of Alfred's spotting him, for he turned back only once or twice to look at the house before striking out along one of the garden footpaths. It was obvious that he had only worried he might be discovered as he left the manor, for once clear of its view, he did not look back again.

Jack followed more swiftly now, and soon perceived that Alfred was making for a summerhouse, a sort of folly made of open brickwork, at the bottom of the rose garden. There was a faint light showing in it, and Jack's heartbeat quickened as he realized that Sudbury must be waiting inside. Alfred, he saw, had paused to take something from his pocket, but he could not make out what it was. He could only hope it was something which would prove the existence of Cecily's father's will. He decided to skirt the beds of roses to another hedge on the far side of the cut-out structure, where he might hear without being seen.

By the time he had taken this circuitous route and approached the summerhouse, Alfred had entered and begun speaking to Sudbury. He was standing near the opening closest to Jack with his back to him, blocking Jack's view of the valet. But Jack could easily distinguish the two men's voices in the stillness. Alfred's was raised to a high pitch, indicating his state of distress.

"But I've already paid you what we agreed upon!" he was saying as Jack crept closer. "How dare you badger me for more!"

"How dare I?" repeated Sudbury, in a tone which showed he would not consent to being insulted. "Oh, I dare all right. I've got a notion to set myself up as a gentleman. Lodgings in London, holidays in Brighton... Why, I might put my name in for a club, with your sponsorship, of course."

Jack could imagine Alfred's livid countenance as he hissed, "You go too far, Sudbury. Remember your position!"

The valet laughed, though he sounded unamused. "You may remember it, your lordship. Or shall it just be 'Stourport' now, between friends?" he added in a scathing tone. "But I aim to forget it."

"But..."

"No more gibberish, my lord! I know very well what sort of fortune you've got for yourself, and it's enough to share easily with me. You've got no heir to spend it on—just your nasty self. Well, you might as well hand me my share and let me enjoy it. I certainly deserve all I can relieve you of for what I did for you."

Jack felt the hair on the back of his neck rise at these words. He moved silently closer, fearing to miss Alfred's response.

But Alfred did not at first reveal the exact nature of his debt to Sudbury. He strove for a reasoning tone. "I acknowledge I am in your debt, Sudbury, and I have compensated you for your service to me. But you cannot go about the countryside, claiming to be my dear friend! You cannot conceive of the ridiculous image you present, cutting up in such a fashion. Your station is stamped all over you. I am perfectly ready and willing to overlook this absurd aberration on your part, and take you back into service, if you will just promise to be a good fellow and stop this nonsense. I could do very well with your services, so..."

"Go back into service with you?" Sudbury's outrage was comical. "And come under that nasty tongue of yours again? No, thank you! I've come for my money and that's what I'll get!"

"I don't have that kind of sum with me just now...." pleaded Alfred, his voice quavering again. But he was interrupted by the impatient valet.

"Then you had better get it, my lord, and fast. I know what you're about here. Come to offer for Miss Wolverton, you have. But I won't allow it! I've divined your scheme! And before you could get married I'd have a little talk with your fiancée. I think she'd be willing to pay me, if you won't, for what I've got. After all, who'd have the fortune then?"

"No! No!" protested Alfred, hysteria rising in his voice. "There's no need to do that! I will pay you, I promise. But if I do, you must promise me to hand over the will!"

Jack's mouth flew open as Sudbury chuckled. So that was it! The valet still had the will. He had never turned it over to his employer.

"And what if I don't, my lord? It is my insurance. I doubt you'll let me starve if I keep that by me."

Alfred's voice was full of venom as he responded, "Why, you leech! I'll not let you bleed me 'til I'm dry. I'd rather die than suffer the worry you've caused me one minute longer."

But the valet was unmoved. "There doesn't seem to be much you can do about it though, is there, my lord? I imagine you shall just have to get used to it."

"Why you damned—!" Alfred started forward and Jack could suddenly see the gleam of moonlight on the object he held in his hand. He leaped from his hiding place and made a grab for Alfred, but not before a shot rang out in the darkness.

As he grappled with Alfred, Jack heard a cry from Sudbury and saw him drop to the floor. Alfred was whimpering in terror from the surprise of being caught in such an action, and although he struggled for a moment, was easily subdued. Before many more moments had passed, Jack was standing over him, holding the gun and catching his breath.

"Now you've done it, my lord," he said, moving cautiously towards Sudbury, who was lying a few paces away. "At this point, you'd better hope that the worst charge you'll be called up for won't be murder." He ignored the cowered baron's feeble protests and stooped to examine Sudbury's wound. The light was poor, but he could make out that it was merely a surface wound, near the elbow. Despite the evident bleeding and the valet's swoon, his breathing appeared normal.

"Looks as if you were lucky," he informed Alfred, secretly relieved not to have a corpse to deal with. "It's only a fleabite. He ought to be awake in a moment and can tell us where that will is."

Alfred stopped his whining and sat up hopefully. "Do you mean to help me get it back? There are two of us now, and only one of him. Together, we ought to be able to make him tell us where it is. He has lodgings in Lombard Street—I've had him followed there. I can lead you to them if you will help me make him tell us where the will is!"

Jack's eyes narrowed. "And then what, my lord?"

Alfred's eagerness revolted him. "I'll make it worth your while! Say, fifty pounds! You're a gentleman! You understand how this villain's been hounding me."

"But what about him?" Jack asked, jerking the pistol in Sudbury's direction. "Won't he talk a blue streak when we've let him go?" He wanted to know just how far Alfred's villainy would go.

But Cecily's cousin was all done in. He moaned, "I don't know what to do. I suppose we ought to kill him, but I cannot be involved in that. You'll have to do it if you want to. This night's work has knocked me up."

Jack could not keep the sneer out of his voice as he said, "No, thank you, my lord. Killing's not to my taste. I only wanted to see how desperate this business had made you. I am not in it for myself—it's Miss Wolverton I'm here for. After your servant revives, you'll both accompany me to London, as you said. We'll recover the will, and I'll bring it back to her."

"Oh, God!" said Alfred in heartfelt despair, but he did not protest. It seemed to Jack that his desire to have the horrible business at an end was even greater than his wish to keep the money. Nevertheless, Jack kept a careful eye on his prisoner until Sudbury awoke, and then made Alfred bind his wound while he watched. The dazed valet was made aware of their plan and was too overcome from the fright he had just experienced to object. Together, the three men slowly made their way to the stables to borrow Sir Waldo's carriage for the journey to London.

CHAPTER FOURTEEN

CECILY HAD GONE to her bed the night before with a heavy heart. Her thoughts had all been for Jack and the unhappy conclusion of their newly formed attachment. She had fallen into a troubled sleep. But the next morning, Cecily was alarmed to discover that both of her guests had disappeared. At first wakening, she knew nothing of this, but when it became clear that neither Jack nor Alfred had come down to breakfast, she began to ask questions. The footman responded that he had not been called to either gentleman's room, nor had Selby been summoned by either one. Only then did Cecily instruct the elderly servant to enter the bedrooms, where he found that neither of their beds had been slept in. Their clothes were still hanging in the wardrobes, however, and nothing in the rooms had been disturbed. But a careful search of their belongings suggested that they had both been dressed to go out. To add to Cecily's discomfort, the head groom came up from the stables to report that one of the carriages was missing along with two of Sir Waldo's best horses.

Cecily went instantly to speak to her grandfather, but Sir Waldo received the news more calmly than she.

"So, Alfred and Sudbury must have had their meeting last night," he said, nodding with satisfaction. "Then we ought to be hearing something soon."

"But Grandpapa!" Cecily protested. "How can we know anything? Jack might be hurt! He did not say anything to us about leaving. And where is Sudbury? Remember there were two of them, and Jack is only one, and limping besides. I cannot receive this news without the greatest anxiety on his behalf. And I insist on sending John down to the village to see whether they've made an appearance."

Sir Waldo tried to discourage her from interfering in Jack's management of the business, but Cecily reminded him with asperity that the matter was entirely *her* affair, and it was Jack who was taking it on with absolutely no call to do so. Indeed, she was so worried about him that she had become illogically angry with him for involving himself in such an unsavoury intrigue.

John, the footman, was duly sent down to the village to enquire at the Rose and Crown, but returned soon thereafter, having learned that Mr. Sudbury had flown the inn as well. He too, it seemed, had left his belongings, which Mr. Rose intended to impound in lieu of payment. This information did nothing to calm Cecily's nerves, for she could only imagine the horror of Jack's setting off with two ruffians. Although she would not have thought of using the term in connection with her cousin or his valet before, now it did not seem so ludicrous.

But she had to agree with Sir Waldo in the end that there was nothing they could do until at least one of the men returned or was heard from. The day stretched, long and uneasy, before Cecily as she tried to occupy herself with her usual pursuits. Her troubled sleep the night before did not help. She had not feared for his safety then, but the long hours spent worrying revealed to her what she had always suspected.

Cecily now knew that her heart had completely surrendered itself to Jack. She loved him as she had never hoped to love. And for the past few weeks, she had grown in the knowledge that he returned her regard, had become so confident of it, in fact, that her future had seemed secure. Then his impossible scruples had arisen to destroy that feeling of confidence. Jack had made her know, just as clearly as if he had said it, that he would not claim her hand until his own fortune was restored. And he had appeared so hopeless as to give her doubt of that event's ever occurring.

Cecily despaired of making a proud, young man see the folly of his pride. She despaired of her own happiness. After all, she could not insist that Jack take her now, poor as he was. She had humbled herself enough in making it clear to him she would have him, no matter what the circumstances. She knew Jack's pride would punish him if he allowed his pity for her to overcome his scruples. And eventually *she* would be the one to suffer. Might he not grow to hate the person who had made him feel less a man than he thought himself?

Cecily even began to have doubts that Jack had any affection for her at all. Perhaps he had been indulging in a pleasant flirtation while he convalesced, not realizing the damage he was doing to her heart. But in truth, she could not deny his affection for her, neither could she be certain of its being deep enough to withstand the passing of time.

Cecily intended to wait. Whether her fortune was restored or not—and she began almost not to wish for it—she intended to stay on with Sir Waldo until Jack could return for her. If he did not, then she would have to deal with her sorrow as it came.

It was with this sad resolution that she continued to wait and hope for word of Jack's safety. But the afternoon only served to increase her fears. The gardener hastened to the house to tell her in tones of great perturbation that he had discovered blood, great quantities of blood, in a pool in the summerhouse. The groom was sent to confirm this finding, and returned to assure her most soberly of its verity.

"Blood it is, Miss Cecily," he said grimly, "though you mustn't think that it's as much as that fool Bob would have you believe." Then he added portentously, "But while I was takin' the time to make sure, I took the liberty of havin' a look round and I found this embedded in the wall behind the summerhouse."

Cecily took the object he was holding in his hand and discovered it was a small nugget of lead. She looked up at the groom in sudden illumination, and he nodded grimly at the sight of her alarm. "That's right, Miss Cecily. That's spent shot, or my name's not Peter Green."

As soon as this bit of news began to be circulated, other evidence poured in. It seemed that many of the servants could claim to having had their sleep disturbed by the sound of a shot, but they had all dismissed it at the time as an errant clap of thunder. Now they were equally certain they had heard a shot coming from the summerhouse.

In great distress Cecily related all this to her grandfather, who listened gravely throughout. "Well, then," he concluded, "we shall either learn that one of the villains has been wounded, or I shall have to start an enquiry."

"Oh, yes! Immediately!" urged Cecily. "You must call out the runners at once. They must be found!"

"Now wait just one moment, Cecy," said Sir Waldo. "There is no need to fly up into the boughs. We can afford to wait another day, at least. Let's give Jack a chance to do his work."

"But Grandpapa!" Cecily protested. "How do we know that it wasn't Jack who was wounded?"

Her voice was clearly unsteady. Sir Waldo, who had been somewhat uncertain of her feelings until now, began to realize there was more to her distress than simply a sense of her own responsibility.

"There, there now, Cecy," he said in a soothing tone, while patting her hand. "There is no need for you to fret for Jack. He's a match for those two popinjays. And besides, our Jack is a clever boy with a clear command of the situation. He would no more brangle with those two ingrates than I would, given half the chance."

But Cecily drew small comfort from these words. The bloodstain in the summerhouse, the evidence of a gunshot, and the disappearance of the three men all said one thing to her: that Jack had been murdered and carried away by the others. What could be more probable than that Jack had been discovered while listening to their conversation; one of the men had shot him—she could not imagine Alfred shooting a pistol so she assigned Sudbury this role—and the two men had fled to avoid being captured?

She blamed herself for allowing him to become involved in her affairs. Her fortune was a curse, and the attempt to recover it had led to misery. But no matter how hard she pled, Sir Waldo would not consent to send for the Bow Street runners. He persisted in thinking Jack fully in command, despite her repeated reminders of his weakened leg.

As the day wore on, Cecily could not bring herself to stir from her grandfather's side. She dreaded the news to come, and she wanted to be near him when it did.

It was in this state of mind that she sat by his bed that evening, pretending to put stitches in her needlepoint. Sir Waldo, to tell the truth, had himself begun to fidget, thinking that if Jack were really all right he would have sent word to them by now. He watched his niece silently, noting the pallor in her cheeks and not deceived in the least by the bending of her head over her work. Leto must have sensed that all was not right, for she raised her head occasionally from the hearth to emit a pitiful whine. Having had enough of this atmosphere, Sir Waldo was about to open his mouth to agree to sending out the alarm, when the sound of coach wheels in the drive stopped him.

Cecily's head jerked up and her eyes questioned him. He nodded grimly.

"There, now," he said. "We'll find out what's been happening before too long."

Cecily rose to her feet and tried to peer out the window, but the night was too dark to reveal anything. Then she tried to resume sitting, but it was of no use. The daylong wait had been too demanding and her nerves were overwrought. She could not stand another moment of uncertainty.

Starting up again, she said quickly, "I will just go see if that's Jack and bring him here to you," and she was out of the door in a second. She picked up her skirts and flew down the hall to the stairs, just as Jack reached the landing. Cecily quickly cupped her hand to her mouth to stifle a cry of relief; grateful tears filled her eyes.

To Jack, after the long night and day of driving to London and back, and the ordeal of dealing with two scoundrels, the sight of his love weeping in distress was too much. He bounded up the remaining stairs, oblivious of the shaking in his leg, and scooped her into his arms.

"Why, Cecily! Dearest love! What is it?" he cried into her hair. She did not respond at once, other than to put her arms about him and hold him as if her life depended upon it. Then, in a confusion of mumbles and sniffs, describing all the evidence that had pointed to his demise, she confessed the extent of her worries about him.

The only answer Jack could produce was to laugh and draw her closer to him before planting a firm kiss on her lips. "So you thought I was dead and gone, did you? Well, I am sorry. I never considered that. I was just anxious to attend to the business and get back to you as soon as possible, and I did not imagine waking the household to announce my intentions would meet with much approval. But I thought you would guess that I had discovered the truth and had gone in confirmation of it."

Cecily raised her face to his with an unspoken question. Jack looked down at her tenderly and brushed a lock of her hair from her brow with a gentle movement of his hand. "Yes, love. I've found the will." Suddenly he remembered his resolve and inwardly cursed himself for his moment of weakness. But it was too late. He had given himself away.

He bent down and gave her one last kiss upon the lips. Then, reluctantly, he pulled away from their tempting sweetness. "We had better go in to your grandfather now," he said grimly. "He will want to hear this as well." He removed his arms from about her and extended one hand instead. After one doubtful, disturbing look, Cecily took it, and the two of them went to join Sir Waldo in his rooms.

Sir Waldo was in a fret by the time they entered, but the sight of Jack was enough to draw from him an enormous sigh of relief. He glanced once at Cecily and saw the confused emotions written on her face, but his eagerness to learn the story caused him to put these aside for the moment. Leto wagged her tail furiously.

"So it was you clattering up the drive," Sir Waldo said by way of greeting to Jack. "I'll admit you had me worried for a bit. I was about to give in to Cecily and send word to Bow Street."

Jack chuckled, but allowed his eyes to stray to Cecily regretfully. "I'm sorry, sir. I had no thought of causing any concern. I knew you would be anxious to have this affair settled as soon as possible."

At hearing these words, Sir Waldo began to question him eagerly, and Jack filled them in on the events in the summerhouse.

"So Sudbury had the will," said Sir Waldo, resting back against his pillows with a grunt of astonishment. "To tell you the truth, I had my doubts you would find anything so important. I thought Alfred would have had the sense to do away with it as soon as possible."

Jack agreed. "I am certain he would have, if he had ever got his hands on the document. But Sudbury must have formed his own plans before they ever left Stourport. He never handed the will over to his master, and the blackmail began as soon as Alfred got back to London."

"I remember," put in Cecily, "that Alfred sent Sudbury ahead with his things. They did not travel together on that occasion."

Jack turned to her and said grimly, "That was Alfred's plan. His only thought at that moment was to get the will safely off your father's property. He did not realize he was giving Sudbury a chance to cheat him."

Sir Waldo snorted. "The only comfort I can get from this episode is the image of the weasely Alfred, done out of his fortune by an unscrupulous servant."

Jack went on to describe for them his adventures of the night and morning. It had taken the two of them to get Sudbury up the stairs to his lodgings, and considerable effort to make him divulge the whereabouts of the will. "By the time we reached London, he had recovered enough from his fright to begin his denials all over again. I had to resort to my own brand of persuasion, while Alfred assisted by holding the smelling salts under his nose."

Sir Waldo gave a reluctant sniff of laughter. "Most gratifying sight, I'm sure. It must have humiliated the dandy immensely to be in waiting on his servant."

Jack did not smile. "Well, whatever his feelings, it did produce this." He put his hand inside his jacket and drew out a wad of papers. Then, gravely, he presented them to Cecily.

She took them, but did not open them, giving Jack instead a look which spoke volumes. Quietly, she moved to Sir Waldo's side and handed him the packet.

"Our thanks to you, my boy," said Sir Waldo, clearly moved. "I cannot begin to tell you what this means to both of us. I can go to my grave now, knowing that Cecily will be taken care of."

Jack refused to allow Sir Waldo to stay in such a serious mood. "There's no need to think of that yet, sir. I made some other arrangements that you might *not* wish to thank me for."

"Oh?" The older man's brow furrowed.

"It's about Alfred," began Jack. "Cecily," he said, turning to her with an apology. "I hope you will forgive me, but I took the liberty of making some suggestions on your behalf."

"Of course I will, Jack," she said, moving closer and giving him her hand. "What is it?"

He took the tiny hand in his and squeezed it before releasing it. "I thought it best to let Alfred make the announcement that the will had been found at Stourport," he confessed. "He has already contacted your father's solicitor and notified him of its existence."

"But . . . !" Sir Waldo rose in protest from his pillows.

Jack held up one hand to silence him. "Please, Sir Waldo. Listen to what I have to say before you make any judgement. I was just trying to avoid another scandal. It seemed to me that this would be the best way to do it."

"But you are going to let that scoundrel go scot-free!" he exclaimed, still not appeased.

"Not exactly," said Jack. "In exchange for this opportunity to save his honour, whatever it's worth,

Alfred has agreed to renounce the title, Baron of Stourport. That ought to open the way for Cecily, or at least her heirs, to regain it at some time."

Sir Waldo lapsed into silence while he reflected on this new development. Cecily's expression revealed the enormous release this was for her, but she smiled sadly at Jack nonetheless.

"And what will become of Alfred, Jack?" she asked.

Jack grinned guiltily. "I hate to admit this in front of your grandfather, but I've another suggestion to make."

Sir Waldo laughed gruffly. "Want Cecily to set him up in his new position, probably. What's it to be? Archbishop of Canterbury?"

"Nothing quite so glorious, sir," said Jack, laughing. "But I do think she might make him an allowance, enough to keep him abroad and out of her way. He's agreed to leave the country provided he has something to live on. Your father's man of business ought to be able to draw something up," he said to Cecily. "You should never be bothered by him again."

"It sounds to me as if Alfred's bargaining, Cecy," inserted her grandfather. "I wouldn't enter into any agreement with that scoundrel if I were you."

She smiled at Sir Waldo and gave Jack a grateful nod. "It will be terribly worth it to me, Grandpapa, never to see Alfred again. You needn't fear I shall indulge him too much, however."

"That's a good girl," said Jack, unable to keep the warmth from his tone. "I wouldn't want to see you deep in another round of court battles. I know you have had enough of such scenes."

Cecily gave a little shudder. "No, thank you. Yes, you are right. I had much rather make Alfred a small annuity than to drag us all up before the courts again. It's time to get on with my life." These last words seemed to recall her to Jack's intentions, and she scanned his face for any sign of them. He refused to divulge anything, however, so she lowered her gaze and moved once again to the bedside.

"And Sudbury?" she asked to cover her hesitation. "I suppose he will go free as well?"

"Yes," admitted Jack. "But do you know," he added with a laugh, "I think Alfred has every intention of taking him on again. He does not go on very well without a valet, and Sudbury suits him quite nicely. They really are two of a kind. Sudbury might prefer another situation, but he's not likely to get one without references. When I left them, they were settling back into their old pattern of master and servant. I had a hard time of it to keep from laughing, but I thought it best not to disturb their newfound harmony. It is only fitting that they should contemplate their exile together. One cannot envy them."

This image did much to restore Sir Waldo's good humour, but a thought occurred to him at that moment which addressed the others' secret concerns.

"And what about you now, Jack? I would like to invite you to stay on with us a while longer. You can hardly think of leaving after doing so much for our benefit." He looked back and forth from Jack to Cecily with a curious frown.

Jack stopped smiling. He could hardly keep his eyes from travelling to Cecily's face, but he knew she was regarding him intently.

"Thank you, Sir Waldo," he said. "But I cannot alter my plans. I must resume my work or run the risk of losing it."

Sir Waldo looked at him in dismay and spoke again in a weakened voice. "Stay on with me, my boy. If your father don't want you, that won't matter. I would be proud to have you as my guest."

Jack's firm gaze faltered at the sound of emotion in the old man's voice. "I . . . I thank you most sincerely, Sir Waldo. That is the greatest compliment you could pay me. But it will not do. I must regain my father's good opinion or I cannot have any opinion of myself." He glanced over at Cecily as he said these words and saw the sadness in her expression. In spite of it, however, she appeared to understand.

All at once, he realized how exhausted he had been by the day's events. Drawing in a deep breath, he turned again to Sir Waldo and begged to be excused.

"I must be off in the morning," he told him. "And I have not had a wink of sleep for two days."

Sir Waldo extended a feeble hand by way of farewell and thanked Jack once again for all he had done for his granddaughter. Jack made a slight movement towards Cecily as if to bid her farewell, but she did not look at him. After a moment's hesitation, then, he said goodbye softly and stepped out the door.

CHAPTER FIFTEEN

AS SOON AS THE DOOR CLOSED behind him, Cecily excused herself from her grandfather and quickly left the room. In a moment, she had caught up with Jack in the corridor and had thrown herself into his arms.

"Oh, little love, you mustn't," he said in an anguished voice, kissing the top of her head and stroking her hair.

"I don't care," she said. She raised her face to his and looked at him defiantly. It was all he could do not to crush her in a desperate embrace. "I refuse to say goodbye in such a public way. I will not be forced into pretending it does not matter."

Jack laughed shakily. "Is the hallway any more private than your grandfather's room?" he asked, deliberately teasing. Cecily blushed at that, but a quick look round satisfied her that no servants were witnessing her bold behaviour. Jack gently removed her arms from about him, but retained her hands in his as he looked down at her earnestly.

"You *do* understand, don't you, Cecily? You know why I must go?"

Her gaze faltered, but she nodded. He could sense the tightness in her throat, for it matched his own.

She spoke in a constricted voice. "I do. But I could not let you go without telling you that I... without knowing whether..."

Jack clasped her to him once again. If he was not certain of having already given himself away, he might not have answered. But he could not leave her wondering if her affection was returned.

"I love you, Cecily. But that is not enough. If I knew if and when my father would take me back as his son, it might be possible. But not knowing when, or even if..."

She raised her face again. He was glad to see that the confession he had just made had restored the confidence in her bearing. "I understand," she said. "But you must also understand that it does not matter to me whether you are Mr. Henley or Jack the Coachman, for I love you with all my heart."

It took all of Jack's character not to respond to this declaration as he yearned to do, but instead, he resolutely put her from him.

"You must promise me one thing, Cecily. That you will not remain here on my account. That you will take up your residence at Stourport and live as you should have been living if Alfred had not robbed you of your fortune."

"My grandfather needs me here," she answered evasively, "and I have no other companion."

"You can hire a companion!" Jack protested.

Then he said in a voice devoid of all hope, "I can be certain of nothing! You must not expect me to come back!"

Cecily lifted her chin high in the air and reminded him, "I have not asked you to promise me anything. And if I choose to go on living here for the time being, then that is my own affair."

Jack gave up his protest and nodded in defeat. Then he released her hands. Cecily was watching him sadly, with eyes rapidly filling with tears. He longed to take her into his arms again for one last kiss, but knew that would weaken him beyond all control. With a hasty goodbye, then, he turned and strode quickly from her, resisting the temptation to look back.

In the morning he rose early and left before anyone else was out of bed.

USING THE EARNINGS he had not yet spent, Jack returned to Birmingham and, after a short wait, took up his old ground on the Birmingham to London mail. He was grateful to have obtained his former position, not merely for the familiarity with which he was greeted by his old acquaintances, but because Davies was still a guard on this route. Only Davies, Jack felt, had some understanding of the disappointment he had just experienced. Not a word was exchanged between the two men about it, but Jack took comfort from the fact that Davies had at least seen Cecily, and had a high regard for her. Jack's own change in spirit was enough to reveal much to the guard, for no matter how much he succeeded in concealing the pain in his heart, there were times when he could not prevent it from showing in his eyes.

Three months of hard work followed his departure from the manor of Sir Waldo Staveley. During this time, Jack did not once permit himself to write to either Cecily or her grandfather, nor did he receive a word from them. It was a great temptation to ask after "the folks up at the manor" when he passed through Hockley Heath, but he resisted. He reasoned that if Sir Waldo had need of him, he knew very well where to find him. But Cecily must not be reminded of his existence if she had chosen to forget her mail coachman. Whenever they passed through the village, Jack never even looked about for a glimpse of them, though his grim visage was the eventual clue that led Davies to divine the whole.

But after three months were up, Jack received a simple summons from his father. The reception of the note caused his heart to beat with anticipation, but he cautioned himself not to assume a reconciliation was nigh. His father might have decided to call him for a number of other reasons; Jack hoped it was not respecting an emergency in his mother's or father's health. In any case, presuming nothing, Jack consulted with the mail contractor, Mr. Waddell, and got his permission for a short leave to call upon his parents.

It seemed very strange to be riding up to his old house on a horse hired in the village. Somehow he had lost his sense of familiarity with the old manor, although he could see that it had not changed. The yew trees still grew right up to the carriageway in front; the ground sloped off in the back to the hay fields and the kitchen gardens. The house itself seemed smaller, but finer than he had been used to thinking it. A surge of pride strangely mingled with humility filled him as he beheld its sturdy Jacobean bricks.

Sir Geoffrey's butler greeted him at the door with ill-disguised joy. Only his amour propre and respect for his station prevented him from giving vent to his feelings on the occasion of the prodigal son's return. With a stiff back, and permitting himself only a small smile, he bowed Jack into his father's library. Lady Henley was nowhere to be seen.

Sir Geoffrey rose from his desk as Jack entered the room. There was an anxious look on his face, and he seemed to have aged since Jack last saw him. For a moment Jack feared that all was not well, and that his mother's ill health was the reason for his summons, but his father's first words reassured him.

“So you've come back, Jack,” said Sir Geoffrey. He smiled with a touch of embarrassment, at the same time letting loose a deep breath. Jack realized at once that his father had feared he would not respond to his call.

“Of course, Father,’ ne answered easily. “You sent for me.”

“Yes, well . . .” Sir Geoffrey waved a hand in a dismissive gesture, as if that worry were now behind him. “I thought it was time we had a talk. Will you be seated?” He indicated a chair in front of him while his expression grew faintly anxious again.

Jack smiled and sat down. He had not been invited to sit on his last visit to this room, he recalled.

Sir Geoffrey cleared his throat and took a chair facing his son. Then he began, "I received a letter some time ago from a Sir Waldo Staveley. . . ."

Jack's head flew up. "Is Cecily—" he began "—Miss Wolverton—all right? Has anything happened to her grandfather?"

But Sir Geoffrey had lifted a hand to put his mind at ease. "No, it's nothing like that, my boy. He does not mention anything of that nature. His letter was to inform me of the service you had rendered Miss Wolverton during your stay in Warwickshire."

Jack sat back much relieved. "Oh, that. Yes," he said.

His father looked at him strangely. "Is that all you have to say about it?" he asked. "You restore a fortune to an heiress, the daughter of a peer, taking your life in your hands to do it, and all you can say is, 'Oh, that?' "

Jack grinned self-consciously. His father's exasperated tone amused him greatly. "What would you have me say?" he enquired with a slight shrug.

Sir Geoffrey did not answer him immediately. He got to his feet and walked a time or two about the room, glancing up at Jack occasionally from under his brows. Finally he stopped and asked Jack abruptly, "Why did you not come to me and tell me of this, my boy?"

At first, Jack did not understand him, but something in his father's grave expression made him reply with the gentle question, "Would you have taken me back if I had?"

Sir Geoffrey sighed. He seemed at once pleased and saddened by Jack's reply. "Would you have understood," he countered, "how hard it would have been for me not to?"

After a pause, he continued, "Jack, Sir Waldo made himself quite clear about his opinion of my conduct in expelling you from the house. I have been holding this letter for the past three months, wondering if you would come to me and use this information to get back in my good graces. But you did not come."

Jack said nothing. Now he understood that his father's sadness was for trusting his own son so little. He looked ruefully down at his hands. His thoughts flew to Cecily and what she might have been doing these three months. She could be in London for all he knew, gaily enjoying the Season.

"You are in love with Miss Wolverton?" The question came at him suddenly, and he lifted his head in surprise.

It was Sir Geoffrey's turn to grin. "Sir Waldo has been open with me about more than one matter."

Jack's eyes lit with a sparkle. "Yes," he answered simply.

"And you would have her for your wife?"

Jack nodded. "But only," he said, "if I could offer her an honourable name."

Sir Geoffrey puffed out his chest, cleared his throat, and took a deep breath. His voice was free of its hoarseness of a moment before. "The name Henley is the most honourable in the land, Jack. I don't see how she could refuse you. Now, I want you to step upstairs and say hello to your mother. She's been fretting to see you these many months. Then, after you notify Mr. Waddell that you will no longer be in his service, I want you to bring your Cecily here to present her to us."

Jack could hardly believe the rapidity with which his father had settled his future, but he sprang willingly from the chair. "Does that mean I am fully restored to the family?"

Sir Geoffrey's extra years seemed to have slipped away as he answered smiling, "Of course, you young jackanapes. Do you think I would invite your young lady here and then put you in the servants' quarters? You had better hurry before she decides to marry somebody else."

Jack sobered, but he was still not recovered from the suddenness of the change in his circumstances. He remembered one more thing that must be settled. "I will bring her here and marry her if you will let me help you manage the estate."

Nothing he could have said could have pleased Sir Geoffrey more. "All right, my boy, if you insist. Now hurry along."

Jack needed no further prodding, but bounded up the stairs to his mother's tearful embrace. There, he tarried for another half hour until she consented to release him, before flying back downstairs to ask his father for the curricle. Sir Geoffrey gave his consent, but to his surprise, Jack did not go upstairs to change, but strode rapidly towards the door.

"Here, boy!" Sir Geoffrey called anxiously after his son. "You do not mean to go after her dressed as a coachman, do you?"

Jack laughed back over his shoulder at his father's sudden demur. "I haven't the time to change, Father. Besides, she might not recognize me if I looked too respectable!"

THE NEXT MORNING, Cecily was interrupted as she was reading aloud to Sir Waldo. Mr. Selby entered and stood before her with a pained expression on his face.

"What is it, Selby?" asked her grandfather, noting the unmistakable disapproval in his valet's demeanour. "Nothing to do with the stables, is it?" Sir Waldo knew his valet's feelings with respect to the outside servants, and suspected the groom had requested to see him.

"No, sir," answered Selby with a sniff. "I have come with a message for Miss Wolverton. It would seem that Mr. Jack has come around to the front door and is asking for a word with her. He suggested she might like to join him for a ride in his curricle." Selby had alighted on this manner of addressing Jack since he could not bring himself to accord him full status.

Cecily had jumped to her feet at the sound of Jack's name, but she recollected herself enough to pause and turn to her grandfather for his permission. Sir Waldo was regarding her with an expression of profound satisfaction.

"Young Jack's turned up, has he?" he said to no one in particular. "Well, you had best get dressed for a ride then, Cecy. I doubt he'll want to be kept waiting."

Cecily blushed and was about to fly to her room for a bonnet, when Selby stopped her temporarily by clearing his throat.

"Pardon me, Sir Waldo," he ventured, "but there is, perhaps, one small matter I ought to mention."

"Well, man! What is it?" asked Sir Waldo impatiently. Leto woke up from a deep sleep and emitted a low growl.

Selby sniffed again, and his displeasure hung so thickly in the air one could almost touch it. Then he announced, "The young gentleman is not properly attired for an outing, sir."

This did cause Cecily to pause, and she looked uncertainly for one moment at her grandfather. But Sir Waldo merely chuckled. "Run along, girl," he said. "If that isn't just like the young rascal. But I expect you to come back within the half hour," he added, to preserve his dignity.

At that word, Cecily flew and, before many minutes were passed, found Jack standing alone by the side of his father's curricle. There was a disturbing gleam in his eye as he bowed humbly to her and, without a word, handed her up into his carriage. Then he jumped in and whipped the horses to a trot, and Cecily's heart skipped a beat as she sensed the suppressed excitement in his movements. But she remained silent until they were well away from view of the manor, and only then did she turn to watch him as he handled the reins.

"Did you go to London?" asked Jack suddenly, when he sensed her eyes upon him.

"No." Cecily flushed with embarrassment.

"To Stourport, then?"

"Once. To see that all was well and to try to restore some order. Many of the servants had been turned off, you see, and I wanted to get them back."

Jack pulled the curricle to a stop under the shade of a large oak tree and secured the reins to the brake. Then he turned and faced her. Her breathing became more rapid as she saw the look in his eyes.

"Will you marry me?"

The suddenness of his question nearly made her swoon for the first time in her life, but she answered readily, "Yes."

Jack let out a loud crow of laughter and took her in his arms, hugging her with pure delight. "What? No questions?" he said. "Do you not even wish to know how or where we shall live?"

Cecily pursed up her mouth as primly as she could under the circumstances and compliantly asked, "Very well, Mr. Henley, where do you intend for us to live?"

Jack's mouth twitched irrepressibly as he looked down at her upturned face. "Oh, I rather thought Birmingham would be a good spot."

"Oh?" she asked unconcernedly.

"Yes," he went on. "It's at the end of my ground. That way, when I come back, you'll be up and can fix my dinner for me."

"How convenient," Cecily agreed. "And what kind of lodgings did you have in mind?"

"Nothing too fancy, I suppose. A room above a shop would be pleasant. Not too far from the butcher for you nor too far from the public house for me."

"It sounds delightful," said Cecily, snuggling comfortably into the crook of his arm.

Jack took her chin in his hand and lifted it so he could stare into her eyes wonderingly. "Good God!" he said. "I do believe you would!"

Cecily answered him seriously. "I think I would, Jack, if there were any need. But I know you well enough to know that you would not be here if your father had not forgiven you."

It was the last thing she was able to say for quite some time, for Jack was so overcome by the love in her eyes that he gave in to his pent-up yearnings and covered her lips with kisses.

After this pleasant interlude, during which Cecily began to know how potent the temptations of the flesh could truly be, Jack clasped her once again to his chest and said, "I've missed you so. And I was so afraid you would not be here when I came."

"But I was," replied Cecily in a shaky voice. "I knew you would come. My trip to Stourport was to ready it for us both when we go to live there—if you are willing?" She waited for Jack's nod, before continuing with a radiant smile, "And Grandpapa knew it, too. He has a great respect for the men of the Royal Mail, you know."

They both chuckled and held on tightly to each other, not noticing the gig that passed them on the road. It was Mr. Rose of the Rose and Crown with his missus, gone to call on her sister who had just been delivered of a new baby.

Mr. Rose, after one look at the two clasped together, put the whip to his horse and hurried on past without a word. Mrs. Rose, who did not at first recognize the pair, turned to have a better look and then let out a shocked cry.

"Why, Mr. Rose! Did you see them two in the carriage? It looked like Miss Wolverton up at the manor and that fellow off the mail—Jack was his name! Did you . . . ?"

"Now, Bertha," cautioned her husband, his visage a mask of disapproval. "You don't have any call to be questioning the ways of the gentry. Though what Sir Waldo would say if he knew, and what the world is coming to in general, I do not like to think!"